Always Never, Rarely Sometimes

By

Alexander Raphael

A collection of short stories

Cover design by Hope Nguyen

Order of Stories

1. The Prankster

2. Lies and Secrets

3. Lucky/Unlucky

4. There, Unthere

5. That Beautiful Girl

6. Motive, Murder, Method

7. The Magic of Christmas

Background Notes

The Prankster

Jimmy Nirvana was and wasn't many things. He was a loner, an oddball and a failed magician. The type that you've probably walked past a million times without noticing. And the feeling would have been mutual.

He had little interest in people but dreamed of being an entertainer and showman. Even if he hated large crowds and crumbled when put under even a smidgeon of pressure on stage. But that was Jimmy. He didn't drink but always told people he was a recovering alcoholic. He didn't smoke but carried cigarettes and a lighter. He was handsome enough but had long convinced himself he wasn't.

Jimmy wasn't approachable, kind or generous either. And certainly not honest or trusting. He wasn't the slightest bit interested in history, the arts or other cultures and was wilfully unable to read a room. And on the rare times he was invited to parties, he wasn't good company, making no genuine attention to listen when people spoke to him and taking far more interest in the room's layout and where he could escape to if there was a fire.

But even if those around him were able to ignore him, he wasn't bothered because he had something else to offer. There was a talent that meant Jimmy was always able to get their attention whether they wanted it or not. He was a prankster. And that, to him, was his own form of magic.

And not just in the half-hearted "Your flies are undone, made you look" or "That deadline was brought forward, just kidding!" kind of way. No. Jimmy Nirvana was a full-on prankster, from as long as he could remember.

Jimmy wasn't sentimental and wouldn't have kept presents from friends or girlfriends even if he'd had any. But he could remember the time when he pulled his first prank. And it was a beauty.

His mother, a quiet, fussy woman who never let her house get untidy, had been given an African fertility symbol by a well-travelled relative after she had struggled to conceive. Despite her stringent scepticism, she was touched by the gift and kept it by her bedside cabinet. And whether science, fate, law of averages or indeed other forces within the statue were at work, she did get pregnant within six months with Jimmy. And his mother believed it was thanks to the statue. Indeed, it was the one item she rarely dusted.

So when Jimmy Nirvana (still just Morris Norman in those days) walked past the carpentry workshop on his way to lunch, he had an idea. There were loose pieces of wood everywhere. He decided to make a rough copy of the statue. He hadn't needed to draw it. It was something that he saw whenever he walked into the living room.

It wasn't too hard to do. The carpentry teacher Mr Garnet even helped a bit, after believing Jimmy's lie that he was making it for his mother's birthday. Jimmy wasn't sure if it was because it was a good lie, whether Mr Garnet had a crush on his mum or else whether Mr Garnet just really liked teaching carpentry. There were times he would think all three in the same afternoon.

And within a few lunch breaks they were able to finish it. It should really have been two but Mr Garnet was a perfectionist and wouldn't accept anything until it was just right. Any time Jimmy tried to cut corners, the 57-year-old teacher would shake his head and stroke his moustache in a slow and serious manner. Over those few hours Mr Garnet told him all about his life, his time at school and his love of woodwork.

But it was time. That same day, an excitable Jimmy got home and decided to play the prank there and then. He waited until his mother was in the next room and then he dropped his statue from the same shelf and screamed out. He had already practised his stunned reaction, but adding water to his eyes from the kitchen tap just beforehand was something he thought of at the last moment.

His mother screamed and rushed to the pieces. She wailed and screamed "Son, what have you done? What have you done?" She started to cry and Jimmy waited for a few extra seconds, before he showed her the original statue.

He was expecting relief from his mother, joy from the fact that something she thought was gone was right here. His father (who two years before had decided to leave without even giving a reason or saying goodbye), had always been losing things. And when he found them, he was happy. At least for a short time. Nothing ever really seemed to make him happy.

But it wasn't relief, or joy, or happiness. Or even appreciation of the imagination of the prank. Instead, it was pure anger. She slapped him. It wasn't hard. His mother was strong in the same way paper mâché was. She was as intimidating as sunlight, scared even by slugs and moths. But the shock of it made it feel like he had been slapped by a wrestler.

She apologised straight away. "Son, I'm sorry. I shouldn't have done that. I don't know what came over me. Please forgive me. I'm sorry." Then she took his hand, kissed his cheek and stared at him right in the eye. "People don't like these silly little jokes. And they won't like you if you do them. You understand what I'm telling you, right? It's important."

And with that she patted the statue and put it back on the shelf before going to her bed to lie down.

Jimmy nodded and stared back at her, but she may as well have been speaking another language. The world was built on jokes. Life itself was one big joke. Why should there be only a set of acceptable ones? Why should he limit his pranks to one day a year? He was thinking bigger.

He hadn't enjoyed the slap but he had enjoyed the feeling of planning the prank. And the buzz of it coming off made him feel alive. Like electricity had jolted through his whole body. The world around him was going to sit up and take notice. He decided to play more jokes to see what would happen, while still working on his magic.

When a new girl joined his school, he told everyone he had seen her and she was really pretty. All the boys waited with baited breath as the teacher heard a knock at the door and the new girl waited to come in. So when she did, short and sweaty, frumpy and fidgety, there was a collective groan as the air of excitement left the room as if by invisible catapult. The girl, pleasant enough beneath all the insecurity, wondered what she had done wrong to be disliked already.

But like his first prank, again a simple one, it wasn't met with a pleasant response. Loser, dork, freak and carnival clown were some of the insults thrown at him. The boys had been disappointed and punched him a few times, as well as throwing his rucksack out of the window. His lunch was squashed, his books were damaged and most disappointingly, his superhero comic was crumpled.

He pretended he'd got her mixed up with somebody else but it made no difference. They had never listened to him or liked him. It was only a few weeks before that those same kids had locked him in the girls' toilet because he had accidentally kicked the only football over the fence during a lunch break. At least for once he had set the agenda. He had made himself be noticed. He had the power. And he was going to keep setting it.

His was an average school. In fact, its motto was the drab slogan "We Keep Trying." But there was one thing the school was proud of. Twenty years before, a 16-year-old student had kicked a penalty from a rather ridiculous 54 metres. The rugby team had been losing 21-0 that day, (which was actually one of their better games) but Jimmy Jackson had seen a shot of glory with five minutes to go and taken it. Rather than kick for touch he had taken on the kick and it landed between the posts. While glory in most schools would have meant scoring the trophy-winning try or beating the division's finest, it was apt that the school's success came within an otherwise mundane annihilation.

But Jimmy, or Kicker as he was nicknamed thereafter, could not have been any more celebrated. Even with his barely average academic skills. When the former "rugby hero" came back to reflect on that moment as part of a 20th anniversary, the first thing Jimmy Nirvana noticed was how the 36-year-old had a crooked haircut, which matched his uneven teeth and slouched posture. But more than his poorly made suit and boring voice, it was Kicker's whole demeanour that depressed him. Even if he had his moment of glory, Kicker was a loser. And deep-down Jimmy knew Kicker was aware of it too.

Jimmy Nirvana made sure to stand up straight when he got a photo later on with the embarrassed centre of attention, who in turn was torn between enjoying the moment and knowing that he had nothing else to show for being an adult.

"Is there anything you would have done differently?" Jimmy asked him.

Kicker looked at him intently and whispered into his ear. "I was nothing. I am nothing. But for a moment I really was something. If you can find those moments, go for it."

And with that, Jimmy was hurried along and Kicker went back posing for photos.

But that advice stayed with Jimmy. He wasn't going to have his life defined by one moment. And as a reminder, he knew he would have to take that rugby ball.

Jimmy had a whole distraction scenario planned, full of intricate cunning. He knew the caretaker (with his jangling keys) always took his lunch at 1 o'clock in the small broom closet where he spoke to his almost deaf mother. Those conversations were hilarious, as the pair had serious issues. He should have recorded them. In fact, Jimmy often found himself impersonating the slogans at home. "I'm not crazy ma" and "Those voices make more sense than yours" were particular favourites. Jimmy half expected to see him on the news one day as part of a grizzly news story.

And he knew the other set belonged to the overweight and rather creepy Mr Belling, or Mr Belching as he was known around the school due to his rather frequent gas problem. Both keys were needed to open the display cabinet. The question of how long each could go without realising it was missing was one thing; the other was when would be the best time to strike and get away unseen.

As it turned out, he didn't need anything half that clever. Staying late one day to read one of his magic books in an empty classroom, he noticed the headmaster's door unlocked. He looked round carefully but there was nobody there. The only sounds he could hear were from the supply room next to it. Mr Belling was not alone. By the angle, he couldn't work out who he was with. At different points, Jimmy had seen Mr Belling hit on each of the female teachers. He wasn't especially choosy.

What was of more interest was the set of keys on the cabinet. Jimmy knew it needed both keys for the glass display case, one red from the headmaster and one blue from the caretaker, as per school policy. This had been brought in after an "incident" regarding the previous headmaster, which was never shared. The locks had changed and the new policy was brought in. But this set actually had both red and blue keys. It made sense the headmaster had secretly made an extra copy; he really was two-faced. Jimmy made sure no one was watching, grabbed them and walked calmly to the display case.

He felt the buzz as he took the ball out and wondered whether to leave something there as a statement. Something that said that not only had he taken it, but something that revealed artistic swagger. But he didn't have the time, the motive or anything useful to put there that he wouldn't miss. Without hesitation, he put the ball in his bag and went home.

The reaction the next day was glorious. There were rumours there had been a scream from the headmaster when he walked past it first thing that morning, that he fell to his knees and shouted "No no no no no no no" and banged his fists on the floor. Others listed him as shouting like a baboon, smashing his fist against a locker and pushing a student to the floor. One version even went that he never noticed it.

The police had been called with a "Big Emergency", and were on the scene within the hour in the rotund shape of the bumbling officer sent over, who was more Clouseau than Columbo. Hapless inquiries were made, the headmaster and other teachers made threats at hastily arranged assemblies, while the religious section offered prayers and pleaded for forgiveness. Yet nothing happened.

Claims were made by different people that they were responsible but that was nothing more than bravado. Jimmy Nirvana did wonder about claiming the adulation but he knew the same kids worshipping the secret thief would rat him out as soon as the cheering had died down. A cash prize had been offered immediately after the investigation hit a dead end. Never trust anyone. They'd just let you down.

After a period concentrating on his magic tricks, he became restless and wanted a new prank. It was time for the Bad Education one. The initial plan was to create a fake set of exam results for different subjects but that would have been too complicated and time consuming. And too greedy when the school was already suspicious. He wanted smaller scale this time around. Besides, he knew which subject to choose.

Mr Sanchez was quite the eccentric. He wore a bow tie, hair flattened as though by an ironing board, and always carried a toy gopher with him. He was also an excellent teacher, being of the hard but fair and extremely dedicated persuasion. Not to mention, rather absent minded. So when a copy of the answers was left by a photocopier no one doubted it. Mr Sanchez had frequently walked off with his briefcase open and more than once his papers had fallen out.

And it wasn't too long before there were groups gathering and hustled voices, with raised voices shushing and jostling within the organised and unorganised chaos.

There was quite the line. Jimmy tried to get a closer look but the crowd only huddled together to ensure he couldn't get in.

"What's going on?" he asked to different kids within the crowd but didn't get a response. He decided to use a different tack. "Well, it's obviously a dirty mag or some form of drugs."

Without looking up, one of the group, a hairy and scruffy individual that had tried and failed to get odd socks going as a trend, mumbled: "Nah, it's a set of answers to one of the tests coming up."

Johnny was dancing inside but he acted all surprised. "Ah nice. Can I get a copy?"

There was a contemptuous shake of the head and tuts from others. "As if it was that easy! Havilah is haggling."

Havilah, an imposing brute who believed in getting his retaliation in first, hadn't read the Bible and had no idea what it meant. He wasn't the slighted bit religious and he sure as hell wouldn't have agreed with any of its teachings. But he had heard the name and liked it and he was influential enough, or rather intimidating enough, that no one was going to correct him.

But it wasn't money he wanted. Whether it was a date, a dare, an errand or even a silly ritual as a form of entertainment, he was in charge. And not everyone was able to, or indeed wanted to, take him up on it. When Jimmy got to the front Havilah just shook his bloated head and laughed.

Well Havilah wasn't laughing when the results came back in. Neither were five of the other 31 who had used the papers, or 20% using Havilah's maths. Jimmy wanted to laugh but that would have been a very bad idea. Havilah was looking for vengeance. Jimmy could laugh enough later. And he did. He even treated himself to a new comic.

Johnny realised that unlike pranksters who revealed themselves afterwards, he didn't need or want that form of recognition. Or indeed risk. As long as he could plan the prank and know of the response, that worked out just great.

But he also realised the pranks that took longer to plan didn't entertain him enough. He needed a quick fix. And so, he started to think about ones that would take less to plan and have a more immediate adrenalin rush.

He had long noticed there was one boy, Sammy, who was always at the local library after his swimming class, around the same time that Jimmy got his magic books. Jimmy always thought of Sammy as a seal. It was all about the way he clapped his hands whenever he laughed that stupid laugh of his. Interestingly, Sammy had been reading one children's fantasy series in particular. Something about a toy robot given magical powers after an encounter with an alien lost from space. He had read all 11 of the series and it would end with the final one, where judging from the cover, Johnny figured the robot and alien finally meet again after years of near misses.

Jimmy made his way to the library's small fiction section earlier than usual. The book was on order but he knew the tetchy librarian (who always wore bad aftershave to try and cover up his drinking problem) had obviously forgotten to save it. With a concentrated look, Johnny quietly went to the book and ripped out the final three pages.

He then grabbed a book near it and sat down to read it, knowing Sammy would come in about 20 minutes with his swimming gear over his shoulder.

As it turned out, it was even quicker as an itchy Sammy came bundling down the entrance stairs, reeking of chlorine. He had obviously been too excited to even shower. Jimmy got a good view as Sammy didn't even bother going to the desk but went straight to the correct part of the fiction section. Picking the book up, Sammy hugged it as though it were a person.

And he went to the front desk as happy as one of those puppies Jimmy's next-door neighbour had just brought back, but Jimmy had let escape. And he was fully unaware that Sammy's laugh would come collapsing down by the end of Chapter 34.

But he wasn't going to be there for the big reveal, which was a shame. Seeing the joy go from their faces was one of the big thrills, knowing they were so helpless and had no idea who to blame. It could be someone they'd never met, or someone they met all the time.

But he had another idea to cater for that. There was a fancy-dress party set in the 1960s that had been advertised for months. They could easily have sold the tickets three times over. What was it with that whole 1960s era, Jimmy wondered?

But at some old diner with bad décor and an over the top 60s vibe, he'd stolen a ketchup container in the form of a tomato. Its shape meant it was perfect for squirting. And when he saw the line of people who wore stylish and original outfits, just about to get off the train station, he made his move.

He looked at them and then pointed behind them, saying "Oh wow, what a costume." The group all looked behind them and that gave him the chance to squirt ketchup all over them. The look as they turned back around just as their outfits were being ruined was joyous. Three of the outfits were mostly dark, but there was one that was white and wow, the red utterly destroyed it. In his notes, Jimmy referred to it as The Ketchup Symphony.

Jimmy Nirvana would have loved to have taken a photo but there wasn't time. Not everyone shared his joy and he had to move quickly. He knew the streets well and was able to escape fine, getting into the crowd and quickly turning his hat inside out and removing his jacket without breaking stride.

"We'll find the weirdo", shouted one of the stiffs he had got a particularly great amount of red on. It was glorious, the shiny-shoed dapper fool not knowing he was standing right in front of the guy he was looking for, just as he headed off on his failed search. How can you find something if you couldn't recognise it even if you could see it?

And all through the times, he was working on his magic. He would try out the tricks, usually the close-up magic kind. He loved sleight of hand, the idea of someone having something but him having the power to remove it without them even noticing it.

But, while he liked the closer deception, he also liked the bigger scale spectacle. And he had a great one planned. He hadn't been to the library since the Seal Trick, but it was time. He had noticed they had a colour photocopier, which worked on an honour system on the odd occasion it was unmanned. And yeah, it was frequently taken advantage of. And that was just fine with Jimmy. It meant it was even easier to get the copies he wanted.

And so, it was time for another disguise. He went heavily bearded in what looked to be a big suit. He wore lifts to make himself taller and wore a fancy hat he had found in a passing charity shop. And he carried himself like someone who had money to burn. And that's what he would do. On the top floor of a high-rise office building from a dead-end estate, he decided to make a speech.

"I've always had money," he said in a booming, theatrical voice. "And my parents had money, and their parents before them. And it's given us nothing but cursed unhappiness. That's why I am going to burn this devil money. Money is wrong. Money is all wrong with the world. Death to capitalism."

Surrounded by the gloom of grey skies that looked like they'd never seen sunlight before and fading concrete eyesores that belonged in a previous century, onlookers were stunned. In a dilapidated building with illiterate graffiti that was all kinds of offensive, stood this millionaire dressed in fancy clothes and throwing £50 notes, burning some of them as they fell to the ground.

"Take it, it's all yours. Money is sinful and your soul is his if you burnish it with riches of ill-gotten means. I am clean. Are you clean? Don't accept the horrors within your soul."

As they scrambled around like hippos at feeding time, crawling around in mud to find the £50 notes that were largely intact, he decided to add some verse. "As it says in scripture. Ecclesiastes 5:10 Whoever loves money never has enough; whoever loves wealth is never satisfied with their income. This too is meaningless."

And with that, he ran down steps and vanished into the shadows, knowing that though the £50 notes would be obviously fake to most people, the human shrapnel scuttling around wouldn't have seen one before. Oh, how he laughed once he was away from the crowds, knowing that their joy was built on illusion.

And as the years went by, different pranks came and went. He listed them all, writing an analysis of each and then having a full ranking. The criteria were broken down into several categories. Length of time spent planning, complexity of prank, expense, suffering of victim and perhaps most important of all, overall feeling when prank came together. In effect, that last category was how he judged the whole prank. And ranking them made him realise that he wanted one where he could enjoy it without needing to run off.

Jimmy had always liked the idea of poison. He knew all about the history of it. And that's why he called his The Nero Effect. He had no interest in killing off his family, or indeed of killing anyone, but he liked the ruthlessness of the former Roman leader. And tramps were so grateful for anything. He'd only added laxatives, but what was great was that each tramp had eaten differently. One had only had a few bites before being ill, another had finished the whole cake almost without swallowing, while the third had waited a while before he ate it. Jimmy wasn't sure if it was fear or anticipation that made the third guy hesitate before eating it, but it had been worth the hour he'd spent hiding.

There was one other joke he'd done more than once. Usually once was enough, but with the right one he could get good mileage out of it. It was listed as Sudden Death. It involved following people for a while and then picking up their habits and routines. It had initially been pretending someone close to them had died. He would pickpocket their phone, type the code he had seen them type in and impersonate their voice telling one of their contacts he was dying. It should have worked better but his mimicry skills weren't as perfect as he'd hoped and it was only the fourth time he felt he'd got it right.

It worked far better as following a woman for a long time and finding out all her habits. And then when she was out with her boyfriend, arrive in disguise and pretend he is dating her. She would be shocked, but he would be able to say lots of facts about her that he wouldn't know from just reading her social media. In his last prank, he'd really done his research. He said they would meet at Jackson's café where they always shared a banana milkshake, how she didn't want him to meet her nosy friend Claire and how she always carried two umbrellas in case she left one behind and it rained heavily.

For Disaster Date to properly work, it needed a strong opening. And with "Hang on, I thought you'd dumped him", it helped get things off on the right track. When he had found out information about the boyfriend it was even better. Believable was better. Both times he had been able to convince the boyfriend. One moment the guy had hesitated after her insistent pleading that she had no idea who this "complete freak" was, but then he had been able to produce her scarf and tell them she'd left it the other night when she stayed over. That clincher feeling was something else.

What he liked about his Book of Illusions, a glamorous title considering magic was only minimally used, was the range of tricks. Even the simple ones gave him plenty of joy. Niagara was about unpicking locks in people's houses and turning all their taps on before leaving, while Gardener's Surprise was making a phone call to the cops that he had seen a body being buried in a back garden. A back garden that had only just been designed with a new set of flowers being planted.

And through the years his mother had always worried he was spending too much time alone in his room. She had even asked two cousins of his to try and get him going to the cinema or the arcade. What was he, 12? His mum had tried herself a few times, but he knew how to get her to stop. He would just have to mention his long-gone dad and she would get sad and go quiet. Why couldn't she understand that magic and practical jokes was what made him happy? In fact, why couldn't anyone understand that?

And it wasn't just her. Her new husband Eugene was now on the scene and was as boring as his name. He was an old man disguised as someone slightly less old. Everything had to sound sage and wise even when it was unasked for and not listened to.

"It's like that moral of the time the lion was captured and there was a lowly little mouse...", "You see son, when Icarus flew too close to the sun…", "That reminds me of this time we went camping and we needed to come together to use teamwork…". The guy was as exciting as dirty bathwater. Him and his mother fit each other perfectly.

He'd tried to have the U2 song "I Still Haven't Found What I'm Looking For" as the song for their first wedding dance, but it wasn't possible. He even thought about paying someone to object to the wedding. But his pranks always worked best when his motives were unknown and he had no connection. That's one reason he never pranked his mother again. He couldn't bear the idea of people finding out and poking around his stuff.

All through school and then college and even university, he'd never been able to tell anyone about his other life. There had been one time he'd felt he'd found a kindred spirit. He wasn't a prankster but he did seem to have a contempt of humans. Fred had been bitter a long time, though he hid it well beneath a layer of sociable cool.

But Jimmy could see it. From his mother's side Fred was from a long line of carpenters, including a failing generations-long family business while his mum worked in the complaints department of the DVLA. Fred wanted to be a musician and had auditioned for drummers for his band Nuclear Playground. His parents kept telling him to concentrate on his studies and get a real job.

Jimmy and Fred had a few classes together and hung out a bunch of times, though it was only in the second year of university they started to interact more. It was Jimmy's first real experience of having a friend. Someone you didn't have to spend time with but you still did. They went to see some football matches at bars, a few films at the cinema and even some stand up. Fred started sharing his love of grunge music too and Jimmy even showed him some of his magic tricks.

After one of the films, where the main protagonist created a fantasy animated world to escape from a bitter divorce (misleadingly described on the poster as an "offbeat comedy"), his friend said to him, "Don't you just wish you were somebody else sometimes?"

The funny thing was, Jimmy felt he already was that somebody else. He had to put on a fake front for society, but he was who he wanted to be. It was that the world couldn't handle him.

He had been tempted to tell Fred and let him in on a few pranks. An extra person would finally enable him to take photos and stay longer to see the person's reaction. Not to mention all the possibilities it offered.

One would be to ask someone which aftershave they preferred. After the bland first one, he would then spray them with some nasty concoction made up of manure and urine and then when they were taken back by him spraying it in their face, Fred could put a rat in their bag. He'd had the idea when his mother gave him some rotten aftershave as a Christmas present.

There was an old neighbour of his who trusted Jimmy with her front door key in case of emergencies. With some very basic sound equipment he could make it sound like she was hearing voices. And one day he could take something over as though he was being nice. He could be talking with her and when Fred started speaking Jimmy would ignore it. Then Jimmy could say he didn't hear anything. That would be a fun one. He'd already named it too. Audio Insanity.

But it never got to that point. After a few weeks Fred came home with Linda, some blonde that was just fake everything. "She seems to really like me," said Fred. "And you know what... I like her too."

And after that he saw Fred less. Fred would still try and make time for Jimmy, but it wasn't the same. Fred was still thinking about her even when he was wasn't with her. Jimmy had been surpassed. He'd met Fred before she had. Why should he be punished? Especially when the traitor could be punished.

So they hung out a few more times and Jimmy made sure he acted all calm. He even joked about whether Linda had a twin sister.

But inside Jimmy was raging. So, for the first time he decided to use his pranks on just one person. The first one was relatively straightforward. Although Fred and him had taken most of the same classes, their exams were at different times. Jimmy knew he could mess up his ex-best friend's exam. He made sure it was just the two of them in the evening, Jimmy helping Fred the night before. When Fred went to get a glass of water, Jimmy changed the time on his phone. He'd seen Fred type in the four-digit code often enough so that wasn't hard. And he'd made sure Fred switched his phone off right after, so his girlfriend Linda wouldn't distract him.

"If you're online you'll only want to talk to her, and that's not a good idea. Switch it off now and go to sleep" Jimmy had said, all sincerity, before going back to his dorm room. The acting was one of the things he enjoyed most about a prank. Like magic, it was part of the illusion.

And when Fred woke up late and missed the entrance to the morning exam, it was glorious. He'd actually missed more than half an hour so he wasn't allowed in. Fred had long carried himself around like he was the coolest. He had his obscure indie band t-shirts and a whole bucketload of philosophy books he quoted from. He even had a funky string bracelet he'd picked up on some "finding myself" trip abroad he always found a way to mention to strangers. And whenever someone got stressed, he'd just say something seemingly profound yet empty, like "It doesn't matter. In life, all that matters is life."

And yet, when he missed the important exam, he was like a spoilt brat not being allowed up past his bedtime. Shouting, throwing stuff, confrontational and yelling: "It's not fair!" He lost his temper so much he was disciplined by the school, made worse by the fact that he had knocked one of the assessors over in his sweary outburst. And his reputation was in tatters with his peers.

He was called a poser and a fake. "I bet he's not even a Nirvana fan," was one of the more damning responses.

But Jimmy wasn't finished. He had thought about disguising cement in the shape of a football so when Fred kicked it, he would break his foot. But that was far too ambitious and impractical. But there was one he could do to rot away more of Fred's life.

By chance, it was Linda's birthday coming up. The distraction had been useful for Fred because he had been moping around but he had perked up when he planned her birthday. First off was the flowers. Fred knew exactly what flowers to get and was beaming as he bought them himself at the florist.

Of course, it needed the "Jimmy touch". In what he noted in his book as the Empowered Flowers prank, he copied the note perfectly but changed the name to a girl Fred had asked out more than once. Mariah had very politely turned him down each time, but there were those at the university who still thought Fred would ditch his "honeybunny" at a moment's notice if Mariah suddenly changed her mind.

So when Fred handed over the birthday flowers to "Mariah", it was a spectacular disaster. Jimmy wished he could have been there, but that would only have been suspicious. Besides, he got a great description afterwards anyhow.

"You think this is funny, do you?" she'd said, increasing in rage. "You think this is some kind of joke? Everyone said you liked her but I thought they were exaggerating. And I gave you a chance and you humiliate me on my BIRTHDAY! Go and find the tramp. Maybe she'll take you. She can have you!"

Fred didn't know what to say, even before she'd thrown the flowers back in his face. He knew he'd written Linda. But when he told his friends, Jimmy included, they each said that it must have been his subconscious. Fred insisted he'd moved on and he didn't even want Mariah now but he wouldn't even get to prove it. Mariah was happy with her guy, the star of the rugby team who would later go up to Fred when out at a bar and tell him to watch it. Fred, aware of the vast difference in strength and build, had to shut up and just stand there with everyone watching.

Jimmy had further pranks planned. He'd had one planned of stealing Mariah's heirloom necklace and then having it fall out of Fred's bag, but didn't get a chance to carry them out. Fred had already decided to quit and go back home.

The situation had taught Jimmy two things. One was that he was a lone wolf best suited to having his own way of doing things and covering his own tracks. The other was just how much he loved to prank people. He had no preference if it was strangers or people he knew.

And over the years he carried out plenty, while also working on his Jimmy Nirvana magic set that he convinced himself he would one day go on stage with.

A prank full of possibilities had been on someone from the office he worked in. She'd been there as long as the peeling walls and chipped mugs. For all her gruff manner, she was a secret author of bad erotica and had sent them off to various agencies. Jimmy had read a copy of *Midnight Supreme* by Emily Everlove and howled at how bad the dialogue was. It was like she'd never even heard of a metaphor, character development or basic structure. It was fun to pretend he was a fan of the book when he called from a fake agency, especially when he'd created a website to back it up. Her excitement had lasted weeks. He thought he'd get her to quit her job before she discovered everything, but though thick, she was surprisingly cautious.

Romantic Switch was another he was fond of. Under one of his many disguises, he would charm some desperate girl he'd see at a coffee bar and then would continue that charm when out at a very fancy restaurant. Right until the expensive cheque came and he was already halfway up the road, dumping his burner phone on the way.

He also liked the idea of doctoring a lottery ticket to make it look as though someone else had won, but life actually did that for him. A proper old school technophobe colleague had asked him to go to the shop to do his weekly lottery numbers as he had to take an important call. Jimmy instead decided to change two of the numbers for the hell of it. And what would you know? The original numbers came in. The guy would have won enough to buy the whole company and every other building on the street.

The rage, the despair, the bitterness was threatening to erupt from the man sat opposite him. And when this downtrodden colleague got violent, his co-workers stepped in. They'd defended Jimmy by saying it was "an honest mistake by an honest guy". And his boss countered it by saying Jimmy hadn't broken any rules and why hadn't he got the ticket himself? Watching his colleague's soul die away over the weeks through knowing his dream was gone was something he had a front row seat for. It was joyous. Even if it didn't really count by the criteria, Lottery Fade may well have been his favourite prank.

And he had plenty more lined up. Work had been busy. One of the reasons his boss had stood up for him. He didn't even have the time to see his mother or new stepdad even if he'd wanted to. He wanted to superglue a bench, send manure to a random stranger through the post and increase the numbers on local speeding limit signs so as to mess up things for motorists.

And he was thinking about all this when he was sitting on a park bench on a quiet Sunday morning. An attractive woman had asked him to look after a heavy suitcase quickly while she went to get a quick coffee. He nodded and thought nothing of it until three minutes later a set of armed police officers asked him to put his hands up and step away from the suitcase. There had been a phone call that the suitcase was full of explosives.

"I don't know what you're talking about. This isn't even my suitcase," he'd said in genuine bewilderment. And yet nobody was believing him and the instructions were getting louder and more forceful.

Jimmy wasn't worried even when he and others were ordered away. But it got serious when a specialist team found a crudely attempted bomb, though not sufficiently well designed to be activated.

His mind swirled as he was bundled into the police car with his hands tied like a common criminal. They'd now be looking for all kinds of evidence. They'd all be rummaging into his flat, his computer, his books, his comics, his ball. And his very precious Book of Illusions.

Who had asked him to look after the suitcase? Was it someone wanting revenge from a prank? Or was it another prankster? Those are very good questions. And those would be very interesting answers.

Lies and Secrets

"Is this seat taken?" the stylish gentleman asked the attractive woman sitting next to an empty chair, whose face was barely visible due to a shawl covering part of her face.

The woman paused for a few seconds. She studied the handsome stranger who stood in front of her before saying slowly, "Jack. Jack Hawthorne. Is it really you?"

Jack paused for a while, going through all the women he had dated in reverse chronological order before finally coming to the right answer. "Anne. Anne Stelkins. Well, who would have believed it?"

Neither was really sure what to say next. What do you say to someone you haven't seen since meeting at an open mike magic show 20 years ago? "Hello?", "Goodbye?", "Much happened?", "I was planning on ringing you but I've been busy for the last two decades?"

Full of confidence after her counselling sessions, Anne decided to start the conversation. "So, what brings you here? If I remember correctly, you don't like coffee bars."

She remembered, thought Jack worryingly. What sort of person recollects that from such a long time? "Well, you are right, I don't like coffee bars, but my girlfriend likes the independent ones and she suggested I come here by myself to check them out." What a pathetic lie, he felt, berating himself. She'll never believe that! She knows why I'm at this singles bar.

Anne was impressed. A girlfriend into quirky coffee bars. Perhaps worth meeting one day. "I'm just here because I heard they have a great selection of coffees and a relaxed atmosphere," she felt the need to say. She didn't want him to find out that she was here looking for a boyfriend. "A guy at work recommended it," she added, hoping Jack might think it was serious.

"So, what work is that?", Jack asked as innocently as he could.

"Accounting," she lied. She was a receptionist at a small business.

"Accounting?" he repeated, pleasantly surprised. Feeling he had to do better, he said he was an architect when in fact he was an approvals officer for his local council.

"I would have thought that you were going to live abroad. Didn't you have dreams of living in South Africa?" Jack said, thinking it better to change the subject.

"I did. I travelled the world for six months. From Cairo to California. It was amazing and the scenery was breath-taking. But there's no place like home." She neglected to mention that she travelled due to a fortunate lucky scratchcard win. "What about you?"

"Only on business. I keep meaning to, but there's always something to be done. Anyway, though, how's the family? Your parents? Jeff? Zappy?"

"They're all fine." Her parents had divorced, Jeff, her brother owned a surprisingly successful pornography shop and Zappy, her beloved Labrador, had died of old age. 15 years ago.

Jack was surprised at her short answer. He figured that they must all be doing well but she did not want to seem arrogant. "Yeah, mine are all doing well." He was not on speaking terms with his parents after a serious argument about responsibility, his two brothers were involved in the loan shark business and he had lost complete contact with all his old friends after drifting apart.

"So how's your life been since I last saw you? It sure has been a while," Anne asked, curious as to what had happened to the guy who had been her first serious boyfriend at 15.

Just what has happened in the last 20 years? Jack asked himself. Caught cold by the question, Jack hesitated.

"Well..., I moved out of my parents' house at 18 and went to university for three years. After that, I ran into an old friend who told me of an architectural apprenticeship I could do at a major company. Academically, I haven't looked back since. In social terms, I've been out with plenty of women but it has never really worked out. Up until recently, of course." He didn't mention his sacking or his month in hospital after being in an unprovoked attack, but apart from the type of job, the rest was correct.

"So you've never been engaged? Married?" Anne asked, interested to know.

"Well, I was engaged and married. In total the relationship lasted six years. But we both realised it wasn't working out. That was two years ago. We didn't have any children." The first wholly honest thing Jack had said since talking to Anne. Only, it was more complicated than that.

Anne wanted to know more. Jack was always so secretive. It was one of the things that she had loved but at the same time hated. No one ever knew what he was thinking. She secretly guessed that he was annoyed that other guys had found her attractive and he couldn't cope with it. Jack was such a jealous guy. She had even found the Roxy Music cover version of the John Lennon song in his room.

Jack had thought about telling her the whole story. It would take a long time. But it would have to be said one day. How he had all that he wanted but it went when he started drinking to deal with the stress at work, which led to more drinking, which cost him his job, which led to him always shouting at his wife, which led to sincere apologies, before the drinking started again and the vicious cycle continued. He had lost control, his job, and his previously stable marriage. When he awoke next to a girl in an area previously unheard of to him, remembering nothing, he knew he had to change. He hadn't drunk since that incident 18 months ago and had landed himself a new job quickly after. But it didn't seem right to tell all this to his first girlfriend.

When asked the same question by Jack, Anne also hesitated, not knowing what to say. "I was offered a job straight after university. They held my job until after my trip and I've been there ever since. In terms of relationships…" She tilted her hand to show good and bad. "I married a guy from work but it didn't work out. We divorced after five years. We both agreed the relationship had run its course." It was all truthful, though there were important parts missing.

The relationship had officially ended five years after marriage, but in truth, it had ended when her husband had started drinking six months after their honeymoon. She had tried to find a reason why, but couldn't. Things had been great before he had started drinking. It was the marriage she had always dreamed of. But once he started drinking, there was no going back. Anne just wished she had realised that earlier. The divorce had been long, bitter and expensive. Fortunately, there were no children to worry about.

Jack had imagined that she would still be married. He hadn't looked at her index finger as she was wearing gloves, but had figured her for the type who needed commitment. They probably just drifted apart but keep in touch regularly, he thought to himself. Happens all the time.

Both simultaneously looked at the clock and realised that they had been talking for longer than they expected. They did not notice each other looking at the time, though they were looking at the same clock.

"I should really be going, it is getting late," said Jack and realised that he hadn't even ordered anything. Still, that hadn't been the reason he had come and he smiled to himself. "It looks a good place so I'll have to come back soon." He stood up and put on his jacket.

Anne was surprised he was leaving as she thought there was more to talk about. But architects are busy people, she reasoned.

Jack had his hands in his pockets but realised he should shake her hand as a means of goodbye. He let out his right hand but ended up bringing a scrap of paper along with it. He always kept junk in his pockets. At the magic show the magician had pulled out all the stuff from his jacket and used it as part of his act.

"Oh, you want my number. I'll just get my pen."

Jack cursed himself for being so careless. Thinking about it, it is good manners and maybe I will send her a message soon.

Anne wrote down the number and, getting up, put on her coat. They both walked to the door and went different ways, each with a smile.

Anne smiled to herself. Even when wearing a heavy shawl, she could still attract men. *He wanted your number.* He still seemed a decent guy and Anne suddenly felt envious of his success. *Perhaps I shouldn't have given him the wrong number.*

Jack grinned. Even women he had dated from the past always remembered him really easily. He had only been interested in the chair to put his feet up. And the notepad was an amusing incident. *And she gave you her phone number. She's definitely still interested.* Remembering her job, he ripped the piece of paper up and threw the pieces into a nearby bin. He could, and would never date anyone more successful than himself.

Lucky/Unlucky

I'm not a lucky guy. I never have been. If anything, I've always been really unlucky. I think it was destined that way.

It goes right back to being a kid. I was the second twin, so everything felt second. People's first question was always, "Who's the oldest?" and my brother would just smile and lap it up. He's always played the big brother, even though we're only a few minutes apart. And as we're not identical, it's always been easy for him to keep up the act.

He got top bunk, first choice of toys and one year, he even got to blow out the birthday candles first. And not only that. He's always had the looks, athletic ability, the charm and the popularity. He could sell sand in the Sahara or ice in the Antarctic. I have a big nose, asthma, a stocky build and a lifetime's struggle with blotchy skin. Not to mention a rather flat, dull voice which somehow becomes high-pitched when laughing. It's always felt like he was just six minutes cooler. My whole life would have been luckier if I'd been the one born six minutes earlier.

But I know what you're thinking. That's not much. Families are complicated, right? Especially siblings. But let me give more examples.

The only thing I had cooler than him was my name. He's Giles, which was a pretty middle-class name for the bog-standard school we ended up at. He always carried it off well but I know he hated it. He'd much rather have had my name: Harry. And yet, as it had to, my name soon became a laughing stock.

You see, my surname is Potter. If I didn't have enough to worry about, I now had an enemy I couldn't even face up to. A literary character who soon became the biggest phenomenon on the planet. And yes, I heard all the jokes. If I was caught trying to sneak into a class quietly, it was "I bet you wish you had your invisibility cloak, Harry!" If I defended myself against being ripped off at the cafeteria it was "Woah there, Harry! I'm not Voldemort." When I missed an empty goal, someone would always cry out, "Shame we're not playing Quidditch." When I fell over and bruised my face, rather than help me up, everyone joked if there'd be a lightning scar. My ginger friend Rob became Ron overnight.

And as there were spells in Hogwarts for everything from memory loss and fetching things to floating and unlocking doors, I was never safe from a reference. One time, the lights went off during an exam and someone shouted that we should use the Protego spell and even the invigilators laughed. Not only was it annoying, but it was wrong. It was the Lumos Maxima spell that created a big burst of light. If I was going to be mocked, it could at least have been done correctly.

Over the years, I tried everything. I tried ignoring it, I tried embracing the joke, I tried mocking others about their names. I even begged them to stop. Nothing worked. Every year there was another book and another updated set of insults.

My first girlfriend was actually called Angela. I joked I should take her surname. She didn't laugh. It turns out her surname was Chicken. Yes, really. My brother found it hilarious. I'd been nervous about asking her out. "Bet you're glad you didn't chicken out," he said as he finished eating his nuggets.

I knew what it was like. Whenever she used a zebra crossing, her friends would joke "That's why the Chicken crossed the road!" She couldn't order chicken or eggs in public or people would joke about which came first. With a birthday in June there were always jokes about being a spring chicken and a bucket list. Even regular nights out with friends would get a hen night reference.

Everyone I knew found it hilarious Harry Potter was dating a Chicken. It was almost a relief to be dumped for a Barry.

"You can get yourself a new bird now," said my cousin without any sense of irony or sense of the progressive world.

At college, my brother (a natural charmer), went out of his way to convince the administrators I had my names mixed around so I was now Winston Harry Potter. I also tried to get people to call me Ringo. Part of a new image. I was a drummer and a Beatles fan, so it seemed as good a nickname as any.

But I was happy with Winston. It wasn't the trendiest of names, but anything was an upgrade. And it felt heavenly. It was glorious. The odd guy would even call me Ringo. But the good times couldn't last. I had my own sliding doors moment.

There were a group of jazz musicians who were so cool it was untrue. Each had that rugged rock star look but had the snazziest dress sense, sharp wit and could speak six languages between them. And boy were they good. It was as if John Coltrane, Miles Davis and Ray Charles had met and formed a band. Even their name was something else. Neon Funkers. I was desperate to be in it. I pestered them so much they agreed I could be their back up drummer.

For six different nights, I sat in the wings. On the seventh, I heard a rumour that a record executive would be attending. He was part of some ambitious new music company and, as the owner was a big jazz fan, they were on the lookout for promising new bands. Neon Funkers' regular drummer had gone to see a friend out of town but his car had broken down, and he'd forgotten his wallet and phone. There was no way he was going to make it on time.

"You're up," the singer told me, his dreadlocks shimmering in the light as he threw me each drumstick. I knew their songs by heart, but more than that I knew how to improvise.

This was my moment. There I was, ready to play for one of the most exciting bands. I breathed heavily to take it all in and then walked slowly onto the stage. And just as the opening song was about to start, I felt a yank on my collar and I was backstage.

"Sorry, short stuff", their out of breath drummer told me between gasps. "This is my time!" And with that he was on, right back in the limelight and playing "Get with the Groove". That's right. That same song that was number one two years later from their chart-topping album *That Special Seventh Night.*

The drummer had been given a lift to the club by a sympathetic driver. This modern-day Father Theresa had actually won a local prize just for being nice. Just my luck! The month before I'd left my coat behind with everything valuable inside. I'd had to walk the three miles back before getting it back the next day. No Mr Nice Guys on that rainy walk back. Forget about Ringo. I was Pete Best, the forgotten former Beatle. At least he'd been on stage with them.

There were other disappointments at uni. An interview with an up-and-coming controversial politician was all ready after months of messaging back and forth. He had all kinds of polarising opinions on everything from immigration to birth control to gun possession. It was going to be sensational. So guess who gets mumps two days before the big interview? A fellow student ended up doing the interview, which was a huge hit and made him an instant star. He had done none of the work but had got all the credit.

And that's not to mention all the birthdays it rained (including one hurricane) either side of wonderfully sunny days, my first car being hit by an escaped bull, joining a company who went bust a month later and actually being struck by lightning.

But things did start to get better. Not long into a new job, I was doing pretty well. I'd joined as an intern but had impressed the right people and I was fully employed and was working my way up the ladder.

"Winston, we're proud to have you in this firm," the boss said as he shook my hand. "We're going places and we want you on that trip with us."

To be fair, my boss at the last place had said something similar before the creditors took over, but even so, this felt different. Unlike my brother, who either held a party on nights out or else just found one, I was quite happy with a low-key life.

I'd even used my untrendy name as part of team building.

After a lot of success with new businesses, we'd lost out on a major client and everyone was feeling down. "Ah well," I quipped. "You Winston and lose some."

There was a big laugh and the mood was lifted. And for once I'd set the tone, not followed someone else's. I was popular. I was having fun. I really belonged. But things weren't to last.

Winston Potter was soon going to hit the news big time. And no, not me. Someone else decided they just had to share their name with the world. Was he some scientist who had made some major breakthrough? Or a humanitarian raising major funds for great causes? Or maybe even a skilled athlete, gifted TV chef or hilariously quick-witted presenter?

No, Winston Potter was a full-time idiot. And even though there were plenty around (and has there ever been a shortage?) he really was a Class A idiot. He probably used the A to spell it. His claim to fame was buffoonery itself. On his YouTube channel, he would film himself falling over and running into things set to silly music. That was pretty much it, but he had built a following. He would even give a couple of soundbites on a few TV shows and did some voice over work for toilet paper, but all in all he wasn't really that famous.

That was until he was asked to be part of a special celebrities' version of a popular quiz show. The aim of the game was to answer 20 questions. Each correct answer was worth £1,000 each, although as this was for charity, they'd increased it to £5,000. As per the regular rules, some were completing a famous phrase, some were multiple choice, some were naming a picture or filling in alternate letters, you get the idea.

In the whole history of the show, no one had ever got lower than six. Most got around 11 or 12. Three contestants had got them all right. Do you know how many Winston got? That's right! Zero, zilch, nothing, nada. He didn't get a single one right. Even with the questions being made easier for the celebrity version. He thought Einstein was an American president, Japan was in Africa, Margaret Thatcher was in Back to the Future and Microsoft sold furniture. The lowest point was arguably when he said World War II began in the 1890s when the question already said World War I ended in 1918.

The headlines were brutal. "Is Winston Potter the dumbest man in the UK?", "Loserton Potter breaks show record with diabolical performance" and "Less than Zero showing by woeful Winston leaves viewers flabbergasted" were some of the nicer ones but social media was especially brutal. Some thought it must be an act. It just had to be. But even those that had worked with him or else just run into him said he was an idiot, giving all kind of anecdotal proof.

"Cheer up bro," Giles told me with reassurance. "At least you're not the world's dumbest Winston Potter anymore," he said stifling a laugh. "You'd at least have got that Japan question right!"

But yet, things would get even worse. A video was leaked of him making disparaging, well let's call it what it was, a set of hugely offensive racist slurs. He did that classic non-apology apology "I'm sorry for anyone offended", with the "not in my character" and "out of context" spiel. The unpleasant idiot was finished but not before he later tried different excuses and dragged the name further down with him.

Even though we looked nothing alike, my social media feed blew up and I had to delete all my accounts.

There it was. A sign from the universe that I had to change my name. None of this would have happened to Embassy Jones, the name I'd have taken if I had been in that funk band. That guy sounds like a boss! But that had just been a pipe dream. I knew my insurance job needed something more traditional. I needed a sensible name for a sensible job. Roderick Thompson seemed as good an idea as any.

There was a place near my office I knew would fix it. I felt doing it in person would be more symbolic, more final. So as soon as I was on my lunch break, I headed over there. The guy was super helpful and I did all the basic forms that would start things in motion. I started to head back but as I was halfway across the road, I heard the name Harry being shouted.

I ignored it but I heard it again. "Harry!" I carried walking before I hear, "Come on, Harry! Don't you recognise me?" Why aren't you turning around?"

I stopped and glanced back only to see a teenage girl waving to some other guy on the other side of the road. And that was all I remembered before the ambulance hit me.

As I found later, the driver was going far too fast. Doctors soon diagnosed I had a fractured leg, three broken ribs, a sprained wrist and numerous stitches to my face. There was some pretty serious damage to my spleen too, which had been the most worrying. It looked like I'd been hit by a bus. Or in this case, a speeding ambulance. The driver was new to the job and had been panicking when made aware the patient was not reacting well to the treatment after a serious heart attack. She barely saw me even after she ploughed into me.

When I woke up, it was obvious I'd been out of it for a while. It was also obvious I should be in a lot of pain but wasn't. God knows what drugs I was on. Amid all the flowers, chocolates, balloons and stuffed toys were my parents, my brother, some nurses and the most beautiful woman I'd ever seen. Even though it was great to see my family, I just couldn't take my eyes off this girl. It hurt to think and some outlines were still blurry, but I didn't remember my twin brother mentioning a girlfriend when we'd last spoken.

"Oh my God, Harry, I'm so glad you're alive!" shouted my mum. Like my dad and twin, she still called me Harry and she only stopped hugging me after I'd audibly winced.

I was still getting used to making out everything all around me. But it was clear from their facial expressions my parents and twin brother had been worried. The girl too, who looked just as anxious as the others. If it were possible, I'd say she had been even more so.

"You had us worried big time, bro," said my brother. "If you'd wanted to get out of work so badly, I'd have forged you a note", he said but without the glint in the eye he usually had when making a quip. It was clear they weren't sure I was going to make it.

It all seemed to go pretty fast after that. The doctors explained in greater detail how the operation had gone. It was complicated medical stuff, even after they tried simplifying it. I was never one for science, so it went right over my head. At five foot three inches, most things did anyhow.

But basically, it had all gone well. I'd got really lucky with the surgeon. He was the best in the city and he was actually heading off on holiday the next day. It was a stroke of luck I wasn't used to. It would still be a while before I was back to where I was, but things felt different.

Rather than feel sorry for myself, I found a lot of things had started to go well. It felt like the last bit of bad luck had happened and that finally my guardian angel had woken up or the wheel had turned or things were balancing up. Whatever metaphor you want to use.

Because over the next few days, the good news kept coming. On the work front, an annoying colleague had decided to change jobs. He'd been insufferably nosy, loud and slow, and they were replacing him with an internal promotion of someone I already got on well with. The company had also decided to expand my department, which meant I would be on some exciting projects and on the way to being fast-tracked. We'd also move to a nicer part of the building, with newer equipment, more space and a better view.

And outside of work, too. After years of fighting relegation, my beloved football team had been bought out by a rich local businessman who had been a fan since he could talk. A whole set of fantastic players were already being connected.

"I am one of you," he'd told the press, not being able to hold back a grin. "I promise you the good times will come back and

I won't stop until they happen. We have been a sleeping giant but we are now wide awake. My dreams are your dreams," he said as he shook his fist upwards. "The future is ours."

If I hadn't still been confined to my hospital bed, I'd have got up on the table and saluted him.

And far more than that. My favourite TV show *Rival Destruction* (which tells of a rich eccentric, who, fed up of the rival team's continued success, decides to buy them out in order to destroy them over a period of time by rotten sales, selling the best players and picking an unpopular former player as manager) was back four years after the writer had a change of heart. It was gripping, funny and thought-provoking and I was gutted after it ended. I couldn't wait to see the new series.

The luck kept coming. The obnoxious local restaurant owner Mr Folker, who regularly swore at disappointed customers was off (yes, yes, insert pun here), after finally getting so many restaurant violations he thought he would be better off moving somewhere new. Antarctica for all I cared. And in its place was going to be a new pizza restaurant. I've always loved pizza.

Even small things from the past had been changing. A box of my favourite toys that had been accidentally given away had been found again at a random garage sale 20 years later thanks to a neighbour with a good memory. A player who I'd lost to in a chess final had finally admitted to cheating (electronic equipment in his ear. I knew it wasn't just an itchy ear beneath his long hair!) which meant I was now school champion. They had told me I could go back to collect the trophy in person as part of the presentation. I could finally say I was a champion. It would now be in the school record books forever.

And you'd never guess who was in the hospital bed next to mine? A former Titan, that's who! Though he had a regular name, to me he was Adrenalin. The same Titan who used to make mincemeat of contestants when they tried to get to the top of the wall before him. Or those who tried (and failed) to beat him on the duelling event or get past him on the aerial rings. He'd got thrown off the show for a couple of ill-advised decisions in his public life, but I'd always liked him. Seeing him again all these years later made me feel like I was 10 again.

He'd only been able to stay for a few hours but my brother and I pumped him for every last question we could.

"Did you date any of the other Titans?", "Do you still speak to any of them?", "Any you didn't get on with?", "Any fights?", "Which event did you like most?", "Did you choose your name?", "Did any of the contestants ever trash talk you?", "How much did you miss it?", "Any hard feelings?", "Have you heard any more about the upcoming reunion tour?"

And my brother and I listened entranced to every answer and every colourful anecdote. What a story we had to tell people. And it got even more incredible when the pin-up of the show, Thorn, showed up, still looking amazing.

We got tonnes more photos and signed stuff which they were happy for us to share. The highlight was a shirt I sometimes still slept in from the show. Now on the back it had Thorn's signed catchphrase just underneath my name, "Not flower time, power time!" and Adrenalin's one of "Infinite Victory". They'd both promised free tickets to the tour that was set to be confirmed, too.

And yet life could get better still. Hours after they'd left and we'd finally stopped talking about them, I remembered I hadn't seen my brother's girlfriend for a few days. Not since the time I woke up actually.

"You haven't argued with your girlfriend, have you?" I asked casually. "I haven't seen her since... actually, not since the operation. Everything good?"

He looked up bewildered. "What girlfriend? I'm happy being out of the dating game for a while." He looked deep in thought for a second before he joined my level of thinking. "Oh, the blonde. The one there when you woke up. No, she wasn't my girlfriend. That's a funny story. Well, maybe you won't find it funny. Me, mum and dad weren't sure whether to tell you."

"Tell me what?" I'd never been patient at the best of times, but even less when I was the only one who didn't know what was going on. Even though I was at the centre of it.

My brother abruptly walked out without saying anything. He did that sometimes. His signature move, he called it. There was a delay of about a minute and then she walked in. I couldn't see her face too well as she had it low, facing the floor. She was nervous and uncomfortable and yet beautiful and the sweetest face I'd ever seen.

"Hi Harry", she said quietly. "You won't know me. I'm Melanie."

She said everything softly, slowly. She kept looking at me trying to gauge a reaction. I looked to see if my twin brother had snuck back in but he wasn't anywhere. Noticing I was looking towards the door she said, "I asked your family to speak to you on my own. I thought it was important I told you myself. I...I...I was the driver of the ambulance. I'm the reason you're here. I'm so sorry."

And with that, she was in floods of tears. You could see how sorry she was, even before she explained all the mitigating factors leading up to it and everything she'd done for me since. As she worked at the hospital, it was her who made sure I got a nicer room, extra attention from the nurses and longer visiting hours. It was her who had made sure the surgeon stayed a day longer to do the operation (covering the costs of the transfer). She'd even been the one who had set it all up with Adrenalin because she found out all about me while I was in the operating theatre. My parents didn't say a word, but my brother had always been a good judge of character and as he once worked as a fast food delivery driver, he knew how crazy the roads could be.

And we kept talking. I told her all about myself (and not just the good points like my twin brother had) and she told me all about herself. She opened up about her pets, her family, how she became an ambulance driver, all the good and bad choices she had made in dating and how they made her the person she was.

And the more she told me about herself, the more I knew I wasn't going anywhere. Being in the hospital bed that would have been the case whatever she said, but I really did mean it genuinely. I had fallen for her big time and it became clear she had fallen for me too.

It wasn't long before I was out of the hospital and back at work. And everything that they say about the birds sounding sweeter and the sun being sunnier was all true. I got back in touch with people I'd drifted apart from and made far more of an effort to make new friends too. I was closer to my family than ever before and was soon making travel plans to go places I had kept putting off in the past. I carried on working hard at work and did get that promotion.

And even if that streak of good luck couldn't last, that was ok. I wasn't planning on going to any casinos or buying any lottery tickets. I already had all the luck I needed.

And that brings us to today. It's been quite the journey but I just had to share it with you. I'm so glad you were all able to make it for our special day. As you raise your glasses, I just have to say this. Melanie, you really have made me the luckiest guy on earth and I can't wait to spend the rest of my life with you.

There, Unthere

The bar was empty, except for an old lady sat quietly in the corner and a scruffy, slightly podgy barman who had mentally switched off hours ago. It was the kind of bar that seemed happiest when empty. Hidden away in a small lane within a crime-ridden area, it was as unappealing from the outside as it was dated, cheap and soulless from the inside. The dark and dirty windows set the tone, as did the mismatching chairs, tacky artwork on the wall and litany of cobwebs. A flickering lightbulb that should have been replaced some time ago only cemented its limitations.

None of these things surprised the 46-year-old walking through the door. There were no niceties as, without looking up, he shouted for a "scotch on the rocks" in a loud and demanding tone. The barman wasn't surprised by the rudeness and reacted the same way as he had all the previous times. He quietly went to pour the drink and told himself that one of these days he would spit in it.

The stick-thin man, with fiery, bloodshot eyes and a hardened face as though formed by cracked concrete, sat down at the table and glanced through a skin magazine and a racing paper. He flicked through the indecent images, but was more focused in who had won big and lost big earlier on and was speculating where he had gone wrong. He was so engrossed in looking at the next day's races that he didn't notice the barman had brought his drink over. He always ordered the same drink whatever bar he was in. He wasn't one for variety.

After making a couple of notations on the paper in front of him, he finally looked up. It was even quieter than usual. The quiet was always welcome, and was one of the reasons he had been drinking here the past few weeks. He hated people. There was only an old woman in the corner. The barman had disappeared. The TV, as ever, wasn't working. Maybe that was why he was missing. Then again, it hadn't been working for weeks.

Within a few minutes, he finished his drink and was wondering whether to stay for another. Suddenly, the old woman limped, tortoise-style, towards his table and sat down opposite him. She plonked down a bottle of scotch. It was classy stuff. The expensive single malt kind. Unopened.

"Here. Let's share it."

Suspicious his whole life, the man hesitated and looked at her intently. She was hunched over like a badly crafted statue, with dry, wrinkled skin, thick glasses that covered most of her face, and a monstrously beige jumper that was at least two sizes too big. She looked boring and useless. Like every old woman. She even wore a ribbon. Who still wore one of those these days?

He paid more attention to the bottle. "This is quality. No one does nothing free. What's the deal, grandma?"

Not intimidated by his glare or his tone, she pressed on. "I bought it as a present for a family member. But he won't mind. And you may as well. The barman won't be back for a bit. Just before you came in, he was telling me that his wife is due any day now. He's left me the keys as he wanted to leave early," she said, taking them out of her pocket and shaking them around.

"To Peter's new baby, whenever it comes," the woman said as she lifted her glass as a toast. The man shrugged and poured a glass. He had never asked the barman any questions. Not even his name. The clown served drinks. There was never any need to know anything about his personal life. As long as he did what he was supposed to, why bother?

Holding his drink in a lazy manner, he looked at this withered old woman again, frail as that crumbling old tree that gets elbowed out of the way by a younger, stronger one. She sure wouldn't make a good bouncer, he snickered to himself. He guessed she was about 80, but she'd had a tough life. She still could have made more of an effort, mind. It was just like she'd let herself go.

The woman swirled the scotch in her glass before she took a little sip. "You're right, this is great scotch. I don't drink much. Not for over 20 years. But this is good. Too strong for me though."

The man was a fan of drinking, but not of small talk. He'd now had two glasses so far this evening and could easily have more, something he often did. He was getting bored though, and there was a match on later. The bottle was just there on the table. There was nothing to stop him just grabbing it and running off. She certainly wasn't going to put up much of a fight.

"I wouldn't do that if I were you."

He stared at her violently, but she didn't blink. In fact, he could see a resolved look of quiet assurance. He had underestimated her. What made her so confident? With just one shove into the wall he could make her into the remains of a crash test dummy.

She smiled. "The place is locked. And even if you do get the keys off me, which wouldn't be difficult I grant you, there is a 6'6, 230-pound surprise waiting for you outside. He knows exactly what you look like, is watching the whole thing on visual audio equipment and is under orders not to let you get past under any circumstances unless given specific permission. He's already had a long day, so I would not push him."

The man was reeling from this huge set of unexpected developments, trying to rationalise her eccentric behaviour. What the hell was she doing? And yes, he did remember that human fridge at the door. Now, that was a guy who would make a bouncer.

But she wasn't finished. She looked him right in the eyes, with a mixture of hatred, satisfaction and relief. "You see, I know who you are Stefan Mitchel."

He knocked the glass over in astonishment. There was nothing left to spill, but the sound was still impressive. He didn't say anything as he instead poured himself another glass hurriedly, in an effort to compose himself.

The old woman wasn't showing any mercy and smiled for the first time that evening. "I bet you wish you had your phone on you now. I know you never take it with you to the pub. You find it disrupting."

To further emphasise the point, she got out her walkie talkie and said: "Hello Eagle. What did I just say? Over."

An immediate reply followed in a controlled, deep set voice. "Yes, I'm here Nightbird. You told him I was in a bad mood because of my long day. You can blame that on a delivery. It was supposed to arrive between 8am -2pm. It arrived at 4.19! And you told him his name was Stefan Mitchel. Over."

He wasn't a chess player, but he knew enough that it felt like he was heading towards checkmate. He'd never liked the game. Took too long and took too much thinking. His mother had tried to teach him as a child but he wasn't a good student. To make the point, he usually flipped the board, winning or losing. But that was the past, and this was the present.

He looked at the old woman for signs of weakness in her demeanour. But there were none. At least for the moment.

Right now, he needed to do something. But he didn't have the upper hand. He'd find out more before he would pounce on any mistake. People always made a mistake. Sometimes it was more obvious, sometimes it was more subtle, but they always made one.

The woman looked at the surroundings before slowly looking back at him. "I'll be honest. It took a long time to find you. You sure like to keep off the grid. You have no connection to your family. No real friends. No roots anywhere. I had to ask a lot of questions to a lot of people to find you. And then hire people to do the same thing, only better."

"Well, I didn't want to be found, did I?" said the embittered man as he slowly pulled out a cigarette. He usually only smoked after he ate, but he knew he could look intimidating and provoke a reaction. He hated rules, and he knew it was banned indoors. But to his surprise, the woman didn't respond.

There was another long pause as the guy pressed his lighter although it took a few attempts. He had a few puffs and the clock on the wall ticked by. The man eventually decided to say something, but as if she could read his mind, the woman broke the silence.

"I know a little bit about you," she said, half glancing at some papers in front of her. "An accountant father, a housewife mother who went back to work when you were eight. No brothers or sisters. Quiet neighbourhood. Your average state school. You got suspended once for fighting and once for cheating in an exam. English, was it?"

He shook his head. "Maths. Fat kid Phelby ratted on me. I got him back later on."

She took out a large folder, filled with all kinds of notes and cut-outs, and started to read from it. "High truancy and left school at 16. In and out of prison for various misdemeanours. A couple of girlfriends over the years. Nothing lasting. One you got pregnant, but don't pay maintenance. You've done different work as you drift around. Construction work. Stable hand. Security guard."

She looked up at him. "Not sure how you got past that security guard background check. Bribery or intimidation, I'm guessing. A couple of waitering jobs abroad." She looked at him without any obvious expression. "That all correct?"

The man nodded, stubbed out his cigarette earlier than he was intending, then went to pour himself another glass. "Close enough. You obviously hired some detective mercenary. Overpriced snitches. How about we reverse the tables? What's your deal? Why am I here?"

She went to speak, but started coughing and calmly took out a well-worn handkerchief. "All in good time. We won't be interrupted. The barman has been paid off. He thinks you're my long-lost son and I've finally tracked you down. Quite sweet, really. Peter really does see the good in people. I used to, as well."

In the distance, a drunk who had stumbled into some garbage bags could be heard shouting at a cat who had been quietly scavenging. Otherwise, it was although the rest of the world had paused, save for the drops of rain which had just started to fall.

"You'll probably think my life is boring," the lady began. She took out a bottle of water and drank from it. "I'm ok with that. I was from a small family. An only child like you. My parents weren't that wealthy by any means, but we were based in the country so I had all the wide open fields to myself. I loved animals. With more money, I like to think I'd have been a vet. I like the idea of healing animals. I had lots of them as a child.

"But while I didn't go to anything as fancy as university, I did go to night classes in the city. I was really good at administration. A natural. I got my qualifications, found a good job and worked my way up to head up my own team."

She checked over to see how intently the man was taking it all in. He had a bored expression but he was listening.

"I'm getting there. This has all been planned. It took me a while to find you, so I may as well take my time. It will make sense soon enough. It's like that time you locked that kid in the cupboard for 20 minutes. You were always going to let him out. You just wanted to make him squirm for a while."

For the first time, the man really did jump out. He even spilt a little of his scotch, and that was something he never did.

His shock soon turned to anger as he jumped up and cursed out. "Who the hell do you think you are, you spinster freak? Where's the double glass in this wretched dungeon?" He paced around the room, his face in thunderous rage, looking for glass. He tapped the walls and, making exaggerated sounds, he let loose his paranoia as though he were a claustrophobic rat.

The old lady was unimpressed and waited until she had finished drinking her water before she began speaking.

"There's no two-way mirror and no one watching other than my security guard friend. Looking for a camera would only waste everyone's time. To your other point, I'm not psychotic, no. I have no interest in psychos. The world would be a far safer world without them. And as I was going to explain before you lost your temper and uttered your nasty language, no, I am not a spinster. And no, this is no game. Games have winners and losers."

Having heard her answer, he realised he needed to calm down. Getting angry was usually effective. Usually, he didn't even have to do anything more. That was enough to scare people, but this woman wasn't as easily intimidated as she looked. He knew he needed to find out more. Right now, she felt she had all the power. Let her think that, then. He'd shut up and let her talk. In a way, it would be funny to let her spend so long setting up her own noose. He'd take extra pleasure from kicking the box out from under her and watching her squirm.

He went to the bar to see what snacks they had. He wouldn't normally eat here, but he was getting hungry. He began to scavenge.

The lady was watching him intently. "I wouldn't bother. They only have ready salted and I know you never eat them," she said in a matter-of-fact tone. He was tempted to eat them just to prove a point, but he really did hate that flavour. Whether she knew it or not, he was also allergic to peanuts, so that was ruled out. He gave a deep breath and sat down.

"So no, I'm not a spinster," she said just before coughing again. "I met George on one of those administration courses. George grew up without much money in his life. His dad had left at a young age and his mum had suffered major health issues, so he had a tough background. But he never complained and instead stepped up. Even as a kid, he took on extra jobs and later put himself through night classes to better himself. He always saw the best in people. A wonderful man. The diagnosis was brutal, but he never felt sorry for himself."

There was a quiet rueful sigh. "It will be two years ago next month when he passed."

The man knew from social conventions that he was supposed to say something like, "I'm sorry to hear that" or "He sounded like a good man", but he never understood it. He'd never met him, why should he care? Besides, in death people always seem better. Like when sports stars retire. They only focus on the winning goals or great performances. Not the times they messed up the big play or got sent off.

"In our 61 years together, we had two daughters. Sylvia and Virginia. I was always a big reader, so it made sense to name them after my two favourite writers. If I'd had a boy, he would have been called Charles."

She took another glass of water, and for the first time that night, she looked wistful. "There were a lot of happy times. We went to the park regularly and flew kites. We had two dogs, Floppy and Barky. The girls went to dance classes. Sylvia played table tennis regularly, but just for fun. She was a natural for teaching. That was her calling. She was always so patient with kids. Virginia loved gardening. And nature. So smart academically, but was always running late and getting lost. And so clumsy, too. She was always knocking stuff over or tripping up."

"We are accidents waiting to happen," the man said out loud, when he only meant to think it. He was clearly rattled. To try and manage the nervous energy, he reached for his cigarette but he knocked the box off the table. The two remaining cigarettes fell onto the already dirty floor. He swore under his breath and decided to leave them. He could only imagine the bacteria in an indoor swamp like this.

The old lady stared at him, but said nothing. The man, fidgeting, poured himself another drink.

"Anyhow, life for 17 years was pretty much perfect," she continued, with more purpose. "Not perfect perfect, but perfect. There were long working hours and expensive bills. George lost his job at one point and things were tight until he found another one. Sylvia needed expensive dental work. Virginia had to have physiotherapy after she fell off a horse. Things were tight at times, but we were happy. So happy. Or at least, we were until the incident." Her vice changed slightly. "And now, we're getting to the reason why you're here."

The woman knew this would get a reaction and made sure to be looking right at him when she said it. The guy snarled as he realised he had underestimated her more than he realised. She was old and sick and mad, but she obviously wasn't stupid. And in his rabid panic, he tried to work out where he had seen her before.

He started thinking more recently, tapping his foot and scratching his face with his long nails. She wasn't from his neighbourhood. He never mugged anyone old. They never carried enough money on them and their phones were always from the Jurassic era. She wasn't from any of the other pubs he had gone to. She wasn't from the dog track or the bookies. Or any of the fast-food joints he'd gone to. For sure she couldn't be a neighbour. She wasn't connected to that woman who was always hassling him for cash for that baby. Could it be one of the kids he'd bullied at school? No, those were always guys. She'd said two girls. Couldn't be a relative of a prison inmate? That was the one place he was well behaved. He was seething that he had no idea. He shouldn't have had those scotches.

He was still thinking as he kept going through all possible places. The old woman was oddly fascinated by his straining expression, as she could see he was going through all the permutations in his head. She waited patiently as he struggled. There was a faint hint of a smile when she could see he was no closer to getting there.

"Alright Mrs Geriatric, where do I know you from?" He was losing his temper, something he'd failed to get to grips with numerous times. "I'll get it if you tell me where from. You want to be here all night?"

The woman tutted. "So rude and aggressive. And so hypocritical. I'm not giving you clues. This isn't a game, remember. And as I've told you numerous times tonight, I couldn't care less about time."

The man's simmering rage erupted as he leapt off his seat and smashed the bottle across the floor. His cheeks reddened and his eyes widened and he screamed out. There was a rummaging of the keys - the door was unlocked. The woman calmly picked up her walkie talkie. "Eagle, no need to come in. He's calmed down. You can back away from the door. Over."

The man sat down, eyes glaring and heart beating with volcanic fury. It was eerily quiet in the room as the man looked at the clock again. The sounds by the door stopped when the security guard moved away.

She waited a few seconds for him to calm down. "There's no need for any more commotion. If you can agree to be civil, we'll continue. If not, we'll wait."

His hatred was still evident, but the fiery rage had left him. At least for the moment.

"There's a reason why you don't remember me," she said in a composed manner. "Before today, we've never met. When you think about it, there's no reason why we would have. The world is a pretty big place, even when we're within the same country. There's 60 odd million of us, all dots moving around in circles. I've read all about your life and there's only one time I can find when our dots overlapped. Just the one. And I wasn't even there. It was when my eldest daughter Sylvia was just walking back to her car one Saturday evening 27 years, four months and three days ago, and left for dead by a hit and run driver. And yes, that driver was you."

The old woman had spoken in a composed way throughout, save for a slightly wobble near the end. Now she had said it, it was out of her hands. This was the one part of the plan she could not legislate for. How would he react? Now he knew why all this was taking place, what would his response be? He'd already gotten mad a few times. But she wasn't worried or afraid. There was nothing perceptive about him. Or particularly intelligent. The world produced dots like him and those dots would continue to cause tragedy the world over.

A slight chill of the wind outside could be heard, as though desperate to squeeze through a crack in the wall and listen in on every last word. "You are wrong, I'm afraid," the man said with a forced show of emphasis. "I've never run over anyone in my life. I've only ever had two tickets, both for parking. This circus has been a disaster. A big waste."

The woman's voice rose a little as she took offence in his response. "Don't insult me. It only makes you look stupid. If you're going to lie to me, Mr Mitchel, please make a better job of it. It isn't two parking tickets, it is three. And you have four speeding tickets. You've also committed the offences of driving under the influence and without insurance."

He scowled. "Fine, you've nitpicked. You've done your homework like a teacher's pet. That don't mean I've done nothing. You half-baked loony."

The old woman let out a long sigh. She went to speak, but coughed. A few seconds after a serious bout of coughing, she started again. "I couldn't care less if you confess. I already know it's you. There's no wire. No trick to get you after all these years. It wouldn't hold up in court anyhow. The guys I paid to find you broke all kinds of rules. Any half decent defence would let you get off easy."

The man was suspicious all his life and wasn't going to stop now. "I won't be admitting nothing. I don't even know the date I'm supposed to have committed this crime."

Said in a distant and quiet, almost robotic voice, the man almost didn't hear her reply. "24 April. It was the day after your 20th birthday. You'd got high as a kite the night before and you went to a club called Dorado's. That same night, you ruined your trainers by throwing them in the mud and hurt your fist by banging on a lamppost. You also screamed at some locals, were sick in some bushes and urinated in someone's lawn. Can't imagine you'd be interested, but the guy who sold you the drugs died of an overdose seven years later. Choked on his own vomit."

The man didn't blink. The truth was, he didn't remember much about that night. Or about that whole period. His late teens and early 20s were a colourful and nonsensical blur. A Molotov cocktail of sex, drugs and waking up in strange and usually trashed flats with no memory of what had gone on the night before. Twice, it had been in a jail cell. Once, it was on the ground outside a casino. He'd had no money other than the odd shift job and whatever he could scrounge off others, as well as the pickpocketing session, but it was good times really. If you've lived life right, you shouldn't be able to remember it.

But if he couldn't remember it, then why should she?

Regaining some composure, he exhaled calmly. "Now, that, was a very long time ago. You've said some things than can neither be proved or disproved. You mentioning some random details is just half a magic trick. And half a magic trick is worthless. Just nonsense. Just like this charade for someone who you needed to move on from a long time ago. Let it go, woman!"

There was a thud as the old woman banged her fist upon the table. For such a frail old lady, it made quite the sound. "It is not nonsense. Or a charade. I'll tolerate things from you. Your coarse language, your attempts at bravado, your selfish, pathetic life when you had so many chances to do some good. But I won't accept wretched, self-serving judgement."

The man jumped. She was old and she was sick. Where had this rage come from?

"I haven't finished. Those detectives looked at your whole life. Not just the murder of my daughter. The whole of it. You've had every chance to be good. Parents who sacrificed everything to give you everything they could. Teachers who tried so hard to inspire you. Employers who gave you every chance. Friends, strangers, girlfriends, court judges. Even the odd cellmate. And what was it all for? You never listened."

"Who's giving advice now?" The man sneered with contempt.

"Not advice", the old woman sighed, before she had another glass of water. "Just observations. I got to know your life pretty well. Not just the accident, though I shouldn't use that word. Not in the state you were in when driving. Witnesses described your brightly coloured car around that time, with that distinctive graffiti you had on it. There's also a description that matched you, and my detectives managed to find the bodyshop where you got your car fixed, to sort the broken headlight recovered at the time. I even found a photo of you with the shirt you'd have been wearing that night, before you had it destroyed. You knew you'd done it."

The man leaned back in a relaxed manner. "You'll never get me on that. You should have spent your retirement years playing Bingo. Not this stupid scheme. What did you think would happen, Miss Marple? That I would just confess? Say how the guilt had been killing me? Nope!" And with that, he started to laugh loudly, which started off like a drunken pirate but then became slower and higher pitched as he laughed himself out.

"No," said the woman with a wide smile. "I assumed you'd drink the scotch. It's clear: among your weaknesses, you're very susceptible to alcohol."

"Wait, what! You put something in my drink?" The man jumped up and went flush as he wondered what it could have been. He didn't feel light-headed. Sometimes, they take a while to kick in. He started rubbing his head energetically and his breathing increased. This went on for a few seconds before he stopped suddenly. "Hang on, the drink was unopened when we met. I remember. It was clear you weren't used to opening Scotch. And your hands shook a lot because you're old."

"You can be observant when you want to be," said the old lady, who was surprised for the first time that evening. "How nice of you to get up when you looked for that spy camera, though. I knew you'd lose your false bravado eventually. And after a couple of drinks your taste buds were dulled a little so it was far more subtle."

The guy opened his mouth wide to shout every obscenity he could think of as loud as he could think of, before the woman quickly put her hand to stop him.

"Save it. I never touched your drink."

The man looked at her intently to see if this was some kind of bluff/double bluff game. He wouldn't put anything past this woman. Desperate people have nothing to lose.

"Don't think the idea wasn't there. I did consider it. There would have been a pleasure in seeing you die. Poisoning would have been a clever way. Not gruesome, not lengthy, but quick, cheap and easy."

The man still couldn't be sure, even if he wasn't feeling any symptoms. He moved the bottle to the other side of the table.

"And the world would be a better place without you," she continued. "Just think of the unfairness of it all. You'll probably live to a grand old age, still getting angry at everyone and making the same mistakes, over and over. And yet, so many good people, who bring such joy, go far sooner. Still... I believe in a greater force. That those who have passed on still look down on us and decide to get involved because they can't stand seeing the pain of those below. My faith got me through the agony of losing her. And again, when my other daughter died, still blaming herself for running late and needing that lift. She was never the same. And George is gone.

"No, all I wanted was the chance to look at you. And explain. I know you bounce around life. You have no roots, no connections. You never see the impact of what you do. All these years later and there's not a day I don't think of that incident. Of what could have been. Of the lives you ruined. I wanted to tell you that the stupid time you were in that car ruined my life."

The man lightly scratched his stomach. He really was hungry. The woman looked at him sadly, but in an unsurprised manner.

"No, this night wasn't about vengeance. I just wanted you to know what it's like to be looking at someone who has lost a loved one. Someone who had something, and just like that, it's all gone. There, unthere, in one moment. There are times when I look up and expect her to walk through the door. And no matter how many times she never does, I keep thinking one day it will happen. Sometimes I'll see someone that looks just like her. Her memory comes alive for a moment. And then a second or two later, you get a better look at the person and it's not them. The memory falls right back. Funny how the mind works."

"Yeah, whatever. Where did you find the goon? Strong, strapping. Built like a bull. He looks useful to know."

"Goon, huh? Some way to refer to him. He can still hear you by the way."

The man shifted uncomfortably in his seat.

"I met him just by being nice about a year ago. He had clearly fallen on tough times, but when I asked him for directions to the nearest newsagent, he was most helpful. He was polite and attentive and actually took me to the place and even helped me when I fell over. He had a kind face. Some people have those. If you look for them, you'll find them. Circles with smiles. I went back to where he was with some sandwiches and a hot drink. We got talking. I came back again with some clothes, some of George's things I couldn't throw out before.

Then I sorted out a place for him to stay and got him a job soon after."

Useful people can be found in all kinds of places, thought the man to himself. He didn't believe in kind faces or kind souls. There were suckers and victims, and it was up to people like him to pounce on both kinds. And beggars were the worst of the lot. Hard luck stories when they were nothing more than street skunks.

He still didn't know why she'd been planning it. And how long she'd had the information. "So why now? Did *Last of the Summer Wine* repeats get ruined when you kept coughing during the punchlines?"

"Well done for realising I'm old. And yes, sick." She took a long breath and coughed a few more times. Lightly at first, then heavier as she could feel her bones shake through her skinny fingers. "There aren't too many days left. The doctors calculated a month at best. I can't see it being as long as that. You know inside you, really. The body is winding down. I want to see George and Sylvia and Virginia again. It's been so lonely without them."

The man stared at her intently, still wondering if he could control her and once again realising that he couldn't. He wanted to see her cry, but the old woman merely coughed a few more times and reached for a handkerchief that had some specks of blood on it.

"It's okay, Mr Mitchel. The evening is over. You can return to what you want."

The old woman picked up a walkie talkie. "Eagle, you can let him through. As agreed, over."

The man sprung up without a second thought. At the door, the same burly gentleman that he had seen earlier was there, putting down the walkie talkie. He looked angry, and stepped in front of him. He opened his mouth to say something. "You worthless piece o..."

"As agreed," interrupted a quiet voice. The lady had stayed in her seat but was watching carefully. The man refused to look up and walked out of the door, his mind trying to make sense of the evening. He kicked a can across the street, leaking the beer everywhere. The nearby tramp heard the commotion and approached, but was scared off by the man's maniacal scream.

The burly security guard chased out after him and then had him by the throat. "In case you were wondering, I wouldn't recommend going to the police. You won't be able to prove anything. Everything will be carefully destroyed and any attention from them would only make them interested in your recent activity. I'd be happy to point them in the direction of your illegal goods "business".

The man scowled off. The security guard went back inside and saw the woman still sat there as though she was the last person left on the planet. It would have made a poignant painting.

Realising the lady would rather be left alone, the security guard didn't say anything. Sometimes there was just nothing to say. He went outside, where he would wait. He would clear up everything after she left, but he was in no hurry. In his life, especially after he'd had to live on the streets, he'd spent a lot of time by himself waiting. There was a purpose here, and he liked this elderly lady.

Lost in her thoughts, she stayed for a while, forgetting about the outside world. As she had for a long time. In her own time, and at her own speed, she got up. She walked slowly towards the door and, surprising herself, did not look back.

A few weeks later, Stefan was waiting in line at an off-license when a burly gentleman bumped into him and handed him a newspaper. The clumsy stranger didn't say anything and was gone before he could get a good look. There were lot of people in the off-license, which was odd for the time of day. He looked at the newspaper instead. It was a local one, so full of dull news about worthless people.

As he opened it up, a grey ribbon fell out. It was the same one the old woman had been wearing. There was also a small part of the newspaper circled. It was in the obituary section. The woman had a name. Doris Robertson. It fit. It was an old person name. And now a dead person name. The couple of lines summed up her life. When she was born, when she died. The family in her life. That she would be buried with the ribbon her daughter Sylvia was wearing when she died in a car accident.

He threw the newspaper and the ribbon in the bin and paid for his drink. He was tempted to get a nice dessert, but they didn't have any good ones. On his way out, he saw the old woman. It was from the back, but he knew that fuzzy hair anywhere. He knew it was a trick. She was just goading him.

Well, it wouldn't work. He grabbed her aggressively from behind and spun her round.

"Ha! So you thought you could…"

But it wasn't her. He had been so sure. He would have bet good money on it. From the height, weight, hair colour and type of hair. Even her posture had looked the same. How odd. When he looked at her from the front, they looked so different.

The stunned stranger stared back at him with an angry face, waiting for an explanation.

Refusing to apologise for his rough behaviour, he walked off. The elderly woman remained there for a few seconds, speechless.

It had been a long day, he told himself. The old bag had made him paranoid. She had gotten inside his head even from the grave. But he wouldn't let it happen again. He was stronger than that.

And yet, over time, he kept running into them. People that looked just like her, but when he went to approach them, weren't her at all. Sometimes the resemblance was more obvious, but other times, he couldn't work out how he had seen something. So, he started to ignore them. But he could never clear it out of his mind. And once or twice they'd approach him, for some banal conversation about the weather, or the length of the queue, or the price of milk. He couldn't escape them. He could not convince his mind at all of the absurdity of it.

He was finding himself distracted. At work, at different pubs, at the hardware store, watching TV. He was even making mistakes at the dog track that were costing him money. One time, he actually thought a hooker he had temporarily bought for the night was wearing that stupid grey ribbon and reacted badly. It had actually just been a lot of silver glitter. He wasn't fussed about how she felt, but her protection sure had been. He was lucky she had asked the guy to stop before he took an even heavier beating.

It was the lack of sleep, too. He tried different pills and different liquids. All colours and all strengths, but nothing was working. So, one night he decided to go for a drive. He'd had some whisky to dry out the medicine, but it hadn't worked. He figured a drive might help. No one was around, so no traffic, and he could listen to the radio. That would relax him.

And as he was out on the quiet roads, it was helping. Being out in his car meant he didn't have to worry about the faces he would keep seeing. In his car, he could go through all the red lights he wanted and at whatever speed he wanted and not have to worry about seeing who was in the other cars. After months, he was feeling like his old self. It was so much easier than driving during the day.

And then he saw her. That long grey hair, that wrinkled skin beneath, that slumped posture, those clothes that were a century old. Walking along the road like a drunk zombie. She'd made it personal now. He'd had enough.

He hit the accelerator. It felt glorious. This woman had been making his life a nightmare. He was going to wipe her out and get his life back.

And in the dawning of the day a few hours later, a combination of police and fire services worked hard together and found the car destroyed, with the driver in pieces, almost like a crash test dummy. There was no woman in sight, not even a ribbon.

That Beautiful Girl

"I'll have a cappuccino, please. I'll be at that table over there by the window. Can you bring it over when it's ready, thanks?"

I'm reading my newspaper as I wait for my cappuccino. I don't know why I am here. It's not my usual hangout. The place I normally go to is being refurbished, but why I picked here instead of any other of the five cafes on the street, I'll never know. I distinctly remember the café as being poor, and it has not changed. The toilets are appalling, the place is filthy, the background music is terrible and the service is abysmally slow. So slow, my cappuccino will be ice-cold by the time the incoherent waiter finds, or rather chooses to find, my table.

As I glance at the headlines on my phone, my facial expression changes from sadness to pity to anger to frustration to disappointment to happiness and then to disgust, as the waiter eventually chooses to bring my cappuccino over. Despite my feelings over my cold "cappuccino", I mumble some sort of gratitude. If my father was here, he'd shout an obscenity before declaring that it be taken back. But my father isn't here, so I start to drink it.

My attention is drawn by a group of young men who enter. The three of them must be in their early twenties. If I was a few years younger or they were a few years older than... then maybe I'd ... Oh, who am I kidding? That would still be too big a gap. I'm far too old for them.

I guess being 58 and divorced for nearly three years with two secretive adult daughters constantly out with boyfriends has made me desperate for a male companion. *They're half your age*, I tell myself.

And shouldn't they be at university? I wonder. It's just gone midday. *Of course they shouldn't*, I angrily tell myself, as a sharp reminder tells me that today is a Bank Holiday and my long-held work ethic orders me to get back to cleaning the house and my notes for the Zelda Fitzgerald biography I am writing.

But I decide to ignore all that and turn my chair to face them. They don't notice me. From the corner of my eye, I then notice a girl entering the café. She is beautiful. She is stunning. She is more beautiful and stunning than I am. Than I ever will be.

I try and convince myself that looks aren't everything, but this denial doesn't last long. However much I will never want to admit it, I know that society will always open more doors for people like her than they do for me.

I watch her as she orders. Immediately, the waiter takes her order. I had to call three times and he never gave me the smile he is giving her. Her drink is ready far quicker than mine. She puts down her phone and starts to drink it. It's obvious she loves it. Either we have different taste buds or the drink was made two different ways. A rhetorical question.

I realise I am looking, staring at her too much and people will begin to wonder, so I turn my attention back to the three guys. I notice their reactions as they see the girl.

"Wow, she's really pretty", says the one who looks the oldest, who has a tanned complexion, trendy haircut, and a band t-shirt that I can't see from where I am.

"Wow, Adrian. You weren't kidding! She is so fit!", says the second guy in total awe, wearing a t-shirt of some cartoon character I don't recognise, that by its tight fit and faded design clearly has been worn far longer than it should have been. "She looks a bit like my last girlfriend, you know..."

He's interrupted by a chorus of laughter from the other two and a set of comments like "Good one Wayne!", "What last girlfriend?" and "That would be Beyoncé right?"

The third of the group is slower to look up and nods his head in agreement when looking over at her. "Yeah, she's nice."

But his eyes go back to his book. He clearly wants to read it, but knows how unsociable that would look. As someone who grew up in her own little library, I can totally sympathise.

"Leave the book alone, Judd," says Wayne. "You can read Steinbeck and his grapes later. You don't see me reading when out in a group, do you?"

"That's because you can't," responds Adrian with a playful tap on the arm as the three laugh.

At that moment, a fourth guy enters the café and waves to them. He's around the same age as the others, though is the only one with a beard and a beanie hat. He's buzzing with energy and actually runs to the table. Just as he's about to reach it he notices the girl and, losing concentration, bashes into a chair and sends several of the drinks knocking. Judd's book is knocked out of his bag, along with several text books and one on how to write a screenplay.

The new guy puts the books back, though not as organised as Judd had them in. He energetically helps clean up the spills with the napkins, but in his haste actually drops more than a few on the floor.

"Wow, have you seen that girl there in the corner?" he says, barely pausing for breath. "You could have told me when I waved to you coming in."

"Something tells me you'd still have knocked all out stuff over," says Adrian with a grin. "Besides Duncan, we're trying to be discrete. Look at her. The last thing a girl like that wants is to be bothered."

At that moment the girl gets the waiter's attention, who immediately goes to her table. She says something to him, but none of us can hear it.

"That sucks, she's going to leave," says Duncan. "I've only just got here."

There is a silence as the group follow the waiter's movements. It isn't a long time, but for the group it is clearly passing in slow motion, even though he is moving faster than he has for anyone else here. When he returns to the table there is a slight gasp. He doesn't bring a bill but a croissant. I can feel the relief of the group from my table.

"You know, this is a sign," says Duncan. "A sign we need to get our asses in gear. She could easily have left and that's it. As long as she's here, we have a chance."

"A chance of what?" asks Judd.

"You know what I mean," continued Duncan. "If we don't go over and say hi, we'll all regret it. We'll wonder what could have been. What she was really like, what if she liked us, all that sort of stuff."

Seeing the group wasn't fully won over, he looked at them more intently. "What does Wayne's favourite namesake say?"

"What's Batman got to do with it?" says Adrian.

"No, not Bruce Wayne!", says an exasperated Duncan. "The ice hockey player Wayne Gretsky. He was seriously good. Anyhow, he once said that you miss 100% of the shots you don't take."

"Even so," ponders Judd. "She probably has a boyfriend."

"Maybe she does but maybe she doesn't" counters Duncan. "But just maybe guys are always too intimidated by her looks to go over and say hi. That means we already have a head start."

The other three think about what he's saying and come round to his logic.

"Duncy boy is right," says Wayne, who is looking intently at her. "She doesn't look like she's waiting for someone. I think she's come alone."

"There is one problem though," says Adrian with a sense of authority. As the oldest he's clearly used to the leadership role. "We can't go all over there at once. It will scare her off.

The easiest thing is if one of us goes over. That way she isn't intimidated or distracted."

"And how do we decide that, then?" says Wayne. "And don't say alphabetical order."

"Yeah, yeah, I get that," replies Adrian as he looks at the table filled with their drinks and a plate of chips left over from whoever was there before. "How about this? There are loads of chips left. Whoever gets the longest one gets to go and talk to her. These things sure look greasy. No wonder there's plenty left."

The other three look at each in silent agreement. It seems as fair a system as any.

"And you can't go more than once" adds Judd. "Or come straight back to the table, as she'll spot us."

"Works for me," says Adrian in response. "Seeing as I came up with the idea, I'll go first," as he moves his hand over the chip and pulls out a rather tiny chip. In fact, it's so small his hand is covered in ketchup. He frowns as he cleans it up.

Judd reaches next. The chip is about three times the size. It would be tough to beat that. Duncan goes next but his choice is a poor one and it's obvious he would be last even if there were a dozen players.

Everyone looks at Wayne who has deliberately waited until the end to select his. With great theatrics he reaches in and pulls out a chip. But it's obvious that Judd has won.

Even from a short time observing them, it's clear that Judd is the quiet member of the group and he's not comfortable being the centre of attention. So I'm not confident when I see him go over to her. It's going to be awkward and painful and I almost don't want to look.

He says "Hi" and she returns it with a friendly smile. There is then an awkward pause before he blurts out in a stuttered voice: "Do you have a light?" The girl looks at him before telling him in a matter-of-fact voice "No. I don't smoke, sorry. But I think I saw that guy by the bar go out for one so he probably has one though."

"Thanks," he says quietly.

Though the girl smiles in perfect politeness, Judd doesn't know what to say.

"You're so... you're really... er, thanks again."

And with that he walks off towards the exit, but the girl helpfully gets off her chair to indicate that the guy he wants the lighter from is by the counter.

The teenagers can't help but laugh at poor Judd after he reappears from the other entrance.

"What happened? You gave up smoking years ago," says Adrian.

"Was that smoking or choking?" says Wayne who laughs so much he is unable to finish his drink.

"I thought I saw one in her bag," replies Judd.

"Come on dude, you totally messed that one up," continues Wayne. "Big time! That was practically a crime scene. Surprised you're not covered in blood."

The other two guys discretely indicate to Wayne not to push it.

"Listen," Duncan says. "You'll get there in the end. Just don't get so nervous. But don't worry, you'll do better if another chance presents itself."

Judd gives a thankful smile before encouraging the group to start the second go.

"OK" says Adrian. "Another decider." He thinks for a moment before his clear green eyes begin to sparkle. "We're lucky. I've actually got a pack of cards on me. Whoever gets the highest card wins. And to throw in a wildcard, the ace is the lowest card."

After he takes them out, the cards are shuffled. "OK, ready," he continues. "You two pick first and then me to prove I haven't cheated. And I can't pick the bottom card."

They each pick a card slowly, almost painfully. The expressive faces of the three add to the tension as they hold their card tightly.

Duncan strokes his beard as he shows his card first. The Ten of Clubs. Wayne then shows his. The Jack of Diamonds. There is a silence filled with the suspense of an object at the highest point about to drop.

The object then hits the ground as Adrian shows his card. The Ace of Spades, which is now the lowest card. Wayne jumps for joy and mocks the two losers.

Adrian then holds his head in his hands as he tells himself, "I shouldn't have added that last sentence. Me and my big mouth."

Wayne gets up, has a quick glance in the reflection of the window, moves his hair around a little and goes up towards her with an exaggeratedly confident stride. I'm really curious what he'll say.

When he gets to her table, she has put her magazine away and is reading *Little Women* by Louisa May Alcott. She is only a few pages in and doesn't notice him until he leans over.

"Hi I'm Wayne and welcome to Wayne's World," he says and laughs. Something tells me it's not the first time he's used that line. Her expression is still blank and you can see her still wondering who he is and why he's come over. Her eyebrow comes up and she looks at him intently. But she shakes his hand anyway and attempts a smile.

"I just had to come over," he continues. "You're reading my favourite book."

She looks surprised. "*Little Women* is your favourite book?"

"Oh yeah, it's brilliant. I can see you've just started so I won't ruin it for you."

"Well actually it's my favourite book too. I've read it half a dozen times. Every time I read it, I'm still so moved," says the girl, whose love of the book lights up her whole face. It's a complete contrast to Wayne, who is trying to hide his panic. He looks to change the subject, but it's clearly a book that means a lot to her.

"Such wonderful characters. Do you have a favourite scene? I read a lot of biographies so Jo's book being burned always jumps out at me. I can totally imagine the betrayal of losing your work like that."

"Oh yeah, it's so moving when his book is burnt. Poor, poor Joe."

"His?" says the girl suspiciously. "You do know Jo is a woman. One of the four main characters."

"Oh right, yeah, of course. That's what I meant."

She looks at him again and the tone in her voice changes. "Humour me. What's the book about?"

Wayne hesitates, caught between giving a vague answer and yet waiting too long before saying something.

"Well... It's about these four friends and the experiences they go through together when they meet at school."

That's not the worst suggestion but I know it's wrong and more importantly, so does the girl.

She sighs in exasperation. "They're sisters, not friends. You obviously haven't read it. Just another liar. I seem to run into them quite a bit at the moment."

Wayne knows he can only make a bad situation worse. There isn't much left for him to say so he heads back. As Wayne gets back to the table via the other entrance, Adrian is arriving with drinks.

"Yeah, she had a boyfriend," Wayne says quickly. "Ah well. We'll head off as soon as we finish these."

Adrian is about to say something but Duncan motions for him to stop and talks instead. "Nice try. You forgot the part about how *Little Women* got you into a little trouble."

Wayne scowls, but the other three laugh. "I'm sure you'll do the "write" thing next time," says Adrian, trying and failing to stifle his laughter.

I look at Judd and he's clearly thinking what would have happened if she had started reading that book before he approached her. I can recognise that inverted shyness though. Something tells me he still wouldn't have gotten her number.

"Fine, fine," says Wayne semi-good naturedly. "Let's see if you do any better."

Adrian and Duncan look at each other as they realise that they have another chance to get to speak to the girl.

"The fairest way is by tossing a coin", says Adrian, who reaches into his pocket and takes one out. "OK, who's going to choose?" he asks.

"Why don't you toss for that," says a slightly moody Wayne.

"I'll choose," volunteers Adrian. "Tails never fails, so tails."

The suspense builds in the few seconds while the coin is flipped and finally revealed.

"Heads."

A sort of sigh and frustrated moan follows as Adrian realises he has lost. "I bet that phrase works with everyone else," he complains before smiling and wishing Duncan good luck. "Good luck, brother. Do the Kerrin name proud."

I am surprised. Brothers? It should have clicked as they do look slightly similar. It's nice to see the sportsmanship rather than the competitive edge though. Duncan thanks his brother, appreciating the support from him, as well as Judd's supportive smile and Wayne's half-hearted attempt.

Duncan moves his beanie slightly as he walks towards her table. Not quickly, not slowly, but comfortably. Not afraid or arrogant but relaxed. He approaches her table and says, "Hi. I was just sitting by myself and I noticed you here. Are you waiting for someone?"

"No, I actually came here to be alone."

"Oh right, I won't bother you," he said without fuss, and turned around to walk back.

The girl looked guilty. "Sorry, that sounded rude. It wasn't meant to. It's just been a really rough few days."

"I'm sorry to hear that. What happened?"

"I got fired on Friday because I messed up on a big project, my pet cat has been ill for a few days so she's been keeping me up and I found out that my now ex-boyfriend has been sleeping with my now former best friend."

Duncan is about to respond when he spots the group laughing and distracted, actually starts laughing himself. He is able to stifle most of it, but the damage is done.

"I'm glad my life is so entertaining to you," says the girl coldly. "I'm not finding it so funny."

"It's not that, it's just..."

But she's not listening and it's clear she wants him to leave. He apologises and leaves her alone. She mutters to herself as she goes back to her book.

When Duncan goes back to the table, he is visibly angry. "You all messed things up for me. I won't forget this!" And with that he's gone before the group can explain. Duncan was so livid he didn't even notice the orange juice dripping all over the table and all over Adrian's shirt, which funnily enough is orange. It reminds me of that line quoted in writing class about overwriting. "The orange was orange."

Adrian goes up to the front to ask for extra napkins but there is no one available so he turns around with a look of enlightenment and actually walks to the girl's table.

"Hi, do you mind if I take these?" he says as he reaches over to grab some.

"Sure, go ahead."

"Thanks," he says drying his t-shirt. "If I have any spare orange juice, I'll put some in the glass."

Despite herself, she half grins.

"I know what you're thinking," he says. "But no, it wasn't a *Notting Hill* move. It wasn't accidentally spilt on me by a random stranger, but a clumsy waiter. I hope your day has got off to a better start than mine."

"Not really," she says before she cuts the sentence short. "I'm not exactly in the singing dancing stage right now so I'll let you go before I pass on my toxic luck."

"You know what, I'll risk it," he says with a cheeky smile. "It's not like they can ruin my shirt any more" he says with a laugh, not seeing the waiter behind him with a pot of coffee. "I'll just bat it away with my invisible bat, that'll do the…"

And with that he catches the waiter and the coffee spills onto him. It's not hot as the waiter was bringing the mostly empty coffee cup back to the counter but it does make a mess on his shoulder and onto his arm.

"Told you!" she says.

He wipes away the coffee and shows her his tattoo. "Its Japanese. It means Embrace Surprises. At least I think it does. The guy assured me it did. I'm telling you; I can deal with anything."

At that moment, a sweet-looking old lady came into the café. She is so unassuming I am probably the only one who notices her. I know what it's like to go unnoticed entering a room. But right behind her comes a huge guy who looks like he could carry a fridge freezer using just one arm. He is angry and intimidating and heads straight towards Adrian's table.

He doesn't wait for them to finish talking. He talks in a quiet voice but with a veiled sense of hostility. "Oi mate, you got the money?"

Adrian looks at him with a mixture of bemusement, bewilderment and just a hint of fear. You don't want to cross this guy. He looks the kind to get his retaliation in first.

"I er, think you have the wrong table."

"Don't play cute with me, funnyboy! Listen, I don't want to get into it with you and your hot lady friend here. But you better have the money the next time I see you, Chuckles. Or else!"

He looks at Adrian intently and though Adrian goes to speak, the man puts a finger to his lips and glares at him. Adrian still goes to talk, but the brooding guy stops him. "I provided the drugs. Now you need to provide the money. You better have it next time I see you, Adrian."

Adrian is astonished at the mention of his name, but before he can say anything, the thug is gone. There is a silence for a few seconds. A long few seconds. The only thing missing is tumbleweed or an elephant in the room.

"I should get going. I was heading out anyhow."

"Hey, I've never met that guy before in my life. I swear."

"If that's the case, then how did he know your name?"

"I don't know, I think he had..."

"A lucky guess, of course," she says with a sarcastic voice. "I think it's best I leave. Yeah, er bye." She doesn't look back at him after she leaves but mutters something about her horoscope had warned her about it being a bad day.

Adrian knows better than to follow her and instead stays rooted in a momentary daze. That's when his brother comes along.

"You messed it up for me, I messed it up for you."

"You mean you did this? You set it all up?

"Yeah sucks, doesn't it? Things being sabotaged by someone close to you. What was amazing was finding someone willing to play along at that short notice. He sure was intimidating. He ended up charging me way more than I had on me. I had to give him my watch too."

"You idiot! We didn't sabotage it."

"He's right," answers Judd. "It was Wayne's fault. He was saying if he was born in Canada like Grestky, he could have pursued a career in ice hockey, as a goalie."

"You've seen my octopus on acid reflexes in air hockey," says a proud Wayne, unaware of the tension. "I always destroy you. Unfortunately, when I went to demonstrate this, I knocked over the juice and wasn't able to stop it before it made a mess."

"Oh right," replied Duncan. "I thought it was like last year when I ruined your jacket and you hid my phone. Or like last week when you blabbed the ending of that book so I..."

"No!" says Adrian with added emphasis before lowering his back to regular levels. "But it's too late now anyhow. She's gone. We should be heading off, too. No point hanging around. Have you seen the bathrooms here? You can see the water all over the floor even from here! At least, I hope it's water…"

They sort out the bill and get up to leave.

Judd looks at them intently. "So, is this a funny story or one we never mention again?"

The other three stop momentarily as they consider the question. They don't say anything while they pack up, so I miss what their answers actually end up being.

I take my time over my coffee as different people come and go. It's nice to lose track of time sometimes. My life is rather ordinary, so a little escape right now is especially welcome. But as the café starts to empty, I know it's time to go back to my mundane reality. Those articles won't read themselves.

At that moment, the girl from earlier walks in. She's realised she had forgotten to pay and then goes to the waiter to pay for earlier. She has her bank card ready, but the waiter tells her the bill had already been paid by the four guys.

As she turns round, she notices me. We look at each other for a moment and she says, "What are you doing here, mum?"

Motive, Murder, Method

Alfred Joseph was a nice man. The type of man who would lend you his umbrella even if it meant he got sodden wet. The kind of guy that would drive miles out of his way to make sure his friends got back ok. Even strangers sometimes. The guy who would always bring far more than he needed to when invited to a party, but wouldn't be annoyed if guests didn't bring anything when he hosted.

Indeed, he was a legend in the small town for his kindness and generosity. When little Bobby Firman broke his leg and missed out on his trip to Disneyland, Alfred was the one who set up a fundraiser and gave generously himself to make sure Bobby could go when his leg was better. When Alfred's competitor for the Best Homemade Lemonade was disqualified through an overzealous technicality, Alfred made sure she was reinstated, even though it meant he lost out on the prize. When the town was voted among the least desirable, Alfred used it as motivation to help change its whole perception. He worked harder than anyone cleaning up the parks, scrubbing off graffiti and helping to improve dilapidated buildings. And smiled his way throughout.

People would ask for his advice all the time and he would never mind, even when he was out shopping or in a hurry. He made so much time for everyone that people often joked that he must have more hours in the day than everybody else. It was that same humour that led people to comment that the town's most popular attraction wasn't the majestic 40-foot arch by the town hall, but rather the short, bespectacled and much-loved Mr Joseph.

Which made the fact he wanted to kill his wife all the more surprising.

The truth was, Mary had been bothering him for quite some time now. All she had done over the past 10 years was complain. When out with her, he spoke too much or not enough. He spent too much time at the office, but wasn't ambitious enough. He was either too tight or too wasteful or too boring or too spontaneous. She even blamed him for the rain once.

And yet, in front of his friends and colleagues, she was sweetness herself. Nothing was too much trouble. All his minor achievements were treated as great successes, his dress sense impeccable, even his jokes were funny. And that included the ones even Alfred didn't laugh at.

"Honey, tell them the one about the hippo caught in the tree," she'd said at a work event just last week, as she playfully held his arm. Two weeks before, she'd asked for the one about the bear who complained about the lousy table service and she laughed louder than anyone. And when his wife repeated a quip that she'd heard from someone else, Mary gave Alfred the credit for it once the laughter had stopped.

"You're a lucky man, hold onto her like the wind," his neighbour had told him with genuine affection. "She's smart, funny, gorgeous – the full package" said his next-door neighbour with more than a hint of jealousy. "You're punching so far above your weight, you should be a boxer," his bemused barber kept reminding him whenever he went in for a cut.

It hadn't always been this way. There had been a time when he looked at her the way the others did.

Alfred could still remember the first time he'd laid eyes on her, even 17 years later. That majestic hair that cascaded like a waterfall, past those fair cheeks and sparkling green eyes. The smile that could have lit up the room if the electricity had gone out. And that pink dress. When he was feeling low after being on the end of Mary's sharp tongue, he would stare at that pink dress and be transported to that wonderful time when it was all perfect.

But those were faded memories now. He got more warmth from his freezer and more joy from a bank statement.

Alfred wanted out. He had done for years. But she wouldn't hear of it. She was from a long line of non-divorcers, going back centuries. There had been any number of unsavoury elements, fraud, embezzlement, all kinds of debauchery and more than likely a murder or two. And yet it was hushed up in the official family papers, helped in no small part, by generous and entirely self-serving donations to local hospitals, libraries and schools.

"I am a Taubinek. Taubineks don't divorce," she'd told him with an air of finality. And no matter what argument he used; she wasn't having any of it. It was almost comical as she clung on to the marriage, as stubborn and uncomfortable as someone wearing a wool sweater at the beach. He told himself he would carry out his threat the next morning, but he never did.

But one day he knew it was time. A guy came in to his dentist's surgery, super nervous, sweating, with posture that would have embarrassed Mr Jenkins, his previous patient who had just celebrated his 81st birthday. Alfred had never seen this new guy before, which was a surprise in itself as he knew almost everyone. But even before Alfred grabbed his scaler, the guy was petrified. It wasn't going to be a quick appointment; the guy's teeth could have been a design for a decrepit rollercoaster track. But throughout the whole cleaning, the guy just held a photo of his wife as support. When he walked him to the reception, his wife was there, smiling. In the same situation, he knew his own wife would have refused to come and just laughed at him.

When he got home that evening and told her it was over, she didn't so much as flinch. In fact, she didn't even pause the show she was watching.

"Go ahead," she'd said coldly, as she put down her crystal cut wine glass and glared at him. "But you'll regret it, doctor. I mean, failed doctor."

He jolted, like she had thrown ice cubes down his back, even though it wasn't the first time she'd insulted his noble profession. He was proud to be a dentist. Sure, doctors could keep you alive, but dentists made you feel good. What was the point of being in good health if you couldn't chew an apple properly? It would be the last insult. He didn't look up as he picked up the phone and started dialling his lawyer. Out of nowhere, she took the phone out of his hands.

"I'm telling you that you'd regret it," she said as she closed the curtains and checked that the maids had all gone home. "We will never divorce," she said as her eyes bore into his with pure contempt. "I would destroy you."

Alfred wasn't fazed. "I don't care about the money, I never have," he replied with genuine feeling. It was true, it wasn't an issue for him. He had a simple background and the butlers and maids seemed unnecessary. And inconvenient. As they were all paid by her, he knew they were all spies who would happily sell him out in a second.

"Oh, I'm not talking about money," as she looked at him intently, this time pausing the show. "I'm talking about your romance with that frumpy waitress klutz."

Alfred let out an audible gasp, but Mary kept talking. "You think you were so discrete, going to all those squalid bars full of repugnant characters and their lecherous ways. You thought you could hide her away and I would be the gullible Stepford Wife. Well, I wasn't going to sit back while you had your wicked way with some doe-eyed tramp with cheap shoes."

Alfred was genuinely shocked. That romance with Polly, the sweet and kind-hearted cocktail waitress, was two years ago, and there was no way she could have known about it. He was beyond discrete. He had covered every eventuality in their three months together. Until one day, Polly came to him and surprisingly broke it off. No real explanation, just that she needed a new challenge and was going to leave town.

"My family has lived in this city for generations. I know every lousy watering hole, every last delipidated pig swill," Mary countered with unfiltered contempt. "How dare you think you could hide things from me?"

"What did you do to her?" It was all Alfred could do to get the words out.

"Ah yes, what happened?" said Mary as she picked up her glass of wine and her smile returned, though the rest of her face was unmoved. "Well, you'll be pleased to know that wide-eyed frump put up quite the fight. She did seem to like you, the poor thing. Wouldn't accept any money and can you believe it, she actually called me the devil? But if feathers don't work, rocks win out. She folded easily when I threatened to expose the "creative accounting" in her father's carpentry business. Some very sneaky pricing. There were more holes in that paperwork than in that heinous attempt at a soufflé you made last week."

Alfred was reeling. He was desperate for her to stop, but she kept talking.

"Think of it like chess. You thought you were in control, but really, I'm the one with all the power. I get to move where I want, do what I want, and you are stuck on your little square, all helpless and pathetic. If you even think of divorcing me, I will move heaven and hell to guarantee your dentistry business goes under and your life is ruined."

Alfred's practice had actually been doing rather well. Business was good and no incidents of any kind. He'd even won a few awards. The right sort of plaque, a joke he always used on his patients.

"I know what you're thinking," she continued, her smile wider and the maniacal gleam in her eyes getting brighter. "But it's rather easy. I have control over enough people who would never dare say no. It just takes a few people saying they reacted badly to your anaesthetic, that you made a lewd pass at them, that you made fun of Mrs Sanders' botched nose operation, that you bribed a judge for the last award, that you cheated on your taxes. Just like that stupid Jenga game you play with your friends. The higher you go up, the easier the wooden pieces fall down and the more mess it is to clean up."

Alfred was struggling to control his varied set of emotions. But by the demented laugh and her frenzied eyes, he knew more punches were coming his way. Just like in the brutal boxing fight his barber had told him about in unwanted graphic detail.

"I actually checked up what she was up to. Apparently, she pined for you quite badly in those first six months. Just stayed in her room and cried. No need to worry, though. She's with a finance banker now. As bland as your Spanish omelette, but she seems happy enough in her new art college."

He tried to switch off at various points as he remembered great times with Polly. The words of his barber kept ringing out. "The guy was out, he was down. And he rose back up like a religious salmon."

Alfred waited a few seconds before answering. Sure, he was taking punches, but he wasn't down. One of the reasons he'd been such a good dentist over the years was staying calm. If something wasn't going right, he knew getting angry or losing control would affect his performance. So, he didn't say any of the things he wanted to say, but instead grabbed the phone back off her.

He started dialling, but rather than try and grab his phone back off him, she walked out of the room. That wasn't like her. Beneath that façade that seemed to fool everyone, she was a cold-hearted schemer.

He'd just dialled the number when she came back. As he heard a voice on the phone, he wasn't really concentrating. Instead, he looked at her and what she was holding. It was a pink dress. The pink dress.

He hung up the phone and looked at her other arm. It was holding a pair of scissors. And before he'd had any time to react, she had started to cut at it. He went to stop her. How could she do this to his favourite dress? She may as well have reached directly inside his head with a flamethrower.

He reached out to stop her, but she put up strong resistance. When did she become this strong? She never worked out and never did anything remotely exerting. Maybe she was the devil, after all.

He wasn't giving up, though, until he had that dress. He tried to grab it, but she kicked him in the shin and elbowed him hard in the ribs. When he reacted in pain, she kicked him with force in the chest. That wasn't stopping him. He got half a finger to the dress, but she bit him on the wrist. He was hurting everywhere, but he was relentless. He almost had it, until her swinging arm caught him in the neck and she used her sharp nails to scratch him on the face. The open scissors fell to the floor.

She couldn't keep up this level of resistance. And yet she was so freakishly strong. As he looked at where the scissors were, she took advantage and now had her arms around his throat. To get her off, he barged her into the table. A loud bang sounded and he could breathe again.

And yet now there was no sound, no fury. It was eerily quiet. Why had she suddenly stopped?

He looked up and saw her lying motionless on the floor with the only movement being the outpouring of red coming from her head. Alfred had never seen so much blood before. It didn't seem to stop. And next to her was a vase he'd bought for her on their honeymoon. It was right next to her lifeless body. He'd even forgotten they had it. And now it was the reason why she was dead.

As he looked back over his shoulder, he saw the pink dress, it was fine, save for a few minor cuts that could be easily fixed. It seemed so unimportant now, when two minutes ago it was the most important thing in the world.

And still the blood kept coming.

Alfred carried on looking and then realising the horror, turned away and shuddered. A moment ago, she was full of life, all too full of life, and now it was like there had never been anything there.

He'd never felt so alone. There was no one he could call or explain the situation to. It really had been an accident but it was still murder and that meant prison. Shame, infamy, incarceration. There was no way he would be able to survive that. He'd barely survived high school.

That meant he was going to have to do something. His brain was going a thousand miles a minute with possibilities, but he was able to block some of them out as he worked out possible scenarios while pacing the room.

Violent burglary? It was a nice idea but not believable. The town was too small for that. There hadn't been a murder in decades or any sort of vicious crime. The local policeman did jigsaw puzzles when at his desk. One of the benefits of living in a dull (if a little untidy) town with nothing to do. There were no creepy admirers or local weirdos to blame it on. Pity, there always seemed so many in the news. He also knew that he would give something away. He watched enough TV shows. No matter how careful they were, there was always something simple that made them crack.

What about pretending that she had gone on an impromptu business trip? She had done it before. Part of her spontaneity and whimsy, he would tell people, but it was just her being selfish and they'd often argued about it. The problem was that while she never told him, she always told the maids. The maids were now away until next week, which gave him some breathing space. But that would involve keeping up that charade for a long time and he wanted it done with.

He could have her fall out of the balcony. That would explain the head injury. But the balcony was locked as they were refurbishing it, so she would never have entered it. He could see why murder was such a specialist area.

Think, think. Something believable, effective and easy. Something that would make him the tragic victim rather than the suspicious husband.

He looked around the room and suddenly thought of the newspaper. There would be plenty of deaths there, being a national edition. He flicked through the pages with frantic zeal. Amidst different news stories, there were all kinds of reasons for death.

Soft drink vending machine guy. Gas explosion lady. Swimming pool drowning. Violent ex-husband. That one was grisly, for sure. Heart attack. Old age. Road accident.

His heart was racing too fast to read it properly. 28-year-old woman carrying groceries. Fast car in residential area. No chance. Hit and run driver. Police looking for witnesses.

That's the one. He could adapt that. Why didn't he think of it earlier? A car accident. She did like to drive fast. She thought she was better than everybody else, so why should she have to wait behind the "plebs" who had a less important life than her? It was the perfect way to kill off his dead wife.

And he knew just the place.

First off, he had to clean up the living room. He went to the garage and hid the rug there (it would have to be destroyed later) and then rearranged the room to make it look as though there was no fight at all. Mary would have approved of the irony, he thought, as he put the vase back on the table and wiped all the blood off.

Luckily, she had died on a rug and not a carpeted area. That made life so much easier. After all the years of misery, it was the least she could have done. Her body was heavier than he thought. Killers never get an even break, he told himself. Or enough credit.

But ultimately, he was able to transport her body to the car without any major hassle. As the car was in the garage, he didn't have to worry about neighbours seeing him, but he was still glad there were no windows. The longer it went on, the more likely it was for something to go wrong.

It was late at night, but he wasn't taking any chances. She was in the boot. If she was alive, he could have imagined her whining. Alfred wryly smiled as he imagined that. Whining even after she was dead. It was the sort of thing she would do.

He got into his simple hatchback. He could have driven her vintage sports car; not like she was going to stop him. He even laughed slightly. But as well as being less ostentatious (the last thing he wanted to do right now was stand out), his was more reliable. Hers had broken down twice in the past year.

As he drove out onto the road, he drummed his fingers on the steering wheel and it all started to come together. He would dump her body at the bottom of the ravine. There was one a bit remote that she drove past all the time on her way to the out of town mall she regularly visited. That would be perfect. He would dump the body there now and tomorrow he would go back with her car at an even more obscure time and go back home in the bicycle he would put in the trunk. It was a clever little idea. Maybe he would have made a good killer.

He listened to the radio as he noticed how quiet the roads were. Just in case anyone recognised him, he wanted to act all natural. It was pretty remote though. He wasn't sure what the right music was to listen to. He just kept skipping the songs. He kept figuring he would find one that felt the mood but he didn't, and he switched it off.

It was probably better to be alert, anyhow. It was about another 20 minutes' drive and he didn't want to be skipping a red light or getting any speeding tickets. He needed to be aware of anyone else, too. A crash would make things awkward, even a minor one.

He hadn't intended to kill her. It was an accident. Self-defence, really. If he'd wanted to, he could easily have done something with one of the many drugs at his office. That would have been quite poetic, the "failed doctor" killing her with something that the average doctor wouldn't trace.

Alfred was trying to stay focused, but his mind was racing about all the opportunities available to him. He had to admit he was glad she was dead. It was freedom. He wouldn't have to hear her nagging again. He could eat in peace, feel good about himself. And the money would be nice. Because of her vast wealth, he'd signed a pre-nup in case of a divorce, but that didn't cover her death. Money didn't motivate him, but who gives back a winning lottery ticket? He was owed it after the good stuff he had done over the years. You do good things so good things come back to you. Why else would you do them?

He could totally play on the sympathy vote. Business might even benefit, too. It was probably too late to get back with Polly, but maybe he could engineer an "accidental" meeting with her. There couldn't be too many art schools around. His mind was swirling. She really was so lovely.

What was that noise?

It was a slight bang. He hadn't seen anything but the car sure had felt it. For the impact it had, it may as well have been an iceberg. With great effort, he was just about able to control the swerving car and get it to stop just before the railing.

He got out in a panic and flustered, spotting shards of glass from a broken bottle. This would ruin everything. He was still away from the ravine. He didn't have a spare in his trunk and he wouldn't be able to make the crash look so effective. And how would he get back?

Stupid bad luck. It was like she was messing with him from the grave. Well, he wasn't going to let her win. This time, he would find a way.

All he had to do was to make the tyre puncture the reason why her car went off the cliff. He'd only just got the car to stay on the road, not the biggest leap that she would have failed and gone off the edge. All he had to do was get her corpse from the boot and into the front with her seatbelt on, swipe a few fingerprints on the steering wheel, readjust the seat and then speed the car over the railing.

He wanted to see what was over the railing. It wasn't as deep as the ravine, but it was effective enough. There were a few trees around and it would be a good few hours before anyone noticed it. By then, he would have time to work out his reaction when they told her she was dead. He wasn't the crying type. The stony silence while he looked into the distance. That would be a good one. He'd need to come up with some excuse about the rug, too.

He could feel a very bright light coming in his direction. If Alfred didn't know better, he'd assume it was a car. And yet it was. Gone midnight. He looked at his watch just to confirm it. Who could be out at this time of night?

As the car approached, he recognised the make. It was a beat-up old Chevy so he knew who it was. It was Eric Dulgan, a middle-aged guy he'd never been close to. Eric's messy divorce had left him rather bitter. He was one of the few who hadn't helped out on his community improvement scheme and kept to himself for the most part. Now though, he had a huge smile on his face.

"Alfred, I'm so sorry, please forgive me," said Eric with genuine sincerity as he looked at the mess made along the road.

Before Alfred could formulate a facial expression, let alone a response, Eric carried on speaking. This was more words than he'd heard him say in the five years he'd known him, and it was like this newly discovered Samaritan was making up for lost time. And what a time to choose. Alfred was gritting his teeth through a fake smile in case he gave anything away.

"It's my fault Alfred," said Eric. I dropped that bottle that caused the flat tyre."

Alfred should have guessed. Eric was always in a hurry, always cutting corners. That didn't explain why he was here though, and messing up his plans. How was he going to get out of this?

"Usually I would have left it," Eric explained with a facial expression as though he'd seen sunlight for the first time. "Someone else would clean it up. But I met your wife earlier today and she was saying such nice things about you. It got me thinking how I never helped you out when you guys were cleaning up the town. That's why I had to come straight back and clean up the glass. Shame about your car. Still, it's not too late to help you out!"

With that, he grabbed the keys from the ignition before Alfred could stop him. "Let me sort this out for you," he said as he walked towards the boot and got ready to open it. "It's the least I could do. Say, how is your lovely wife, anyhow?"

The Magic of Christmas

"And above all, watch with glittering eyes the whole world around you because the greatest secrets are always hidden in the most unlikely places. Those who don't believe in magic will never find it." Roald Dahl

The magic of Christmas was everywhere and the snowy wonderland was happy to share it with everyone and everything. Houses and shop windows were alive as they were lit up in a fantastic array of colours and designs. Intricate lighting decorations, carefully prepared store displays and lovingly made snowmen merged with novelty Santa feet sticking out of chimneys and miniature reindeer antlers, with bright red noses on everything from garage doors to festively decorated garden gnomes.

Carollers were in fine voice as they sang through all the classics, kept warm in the snow with thick novelty festive jumpers, a thermos of hot chocolate and the satisfaction of adding another year to their much-loved tradition. A large Christmas tree, the town's largest ever, shone like a green lighthouse in the centre and brought smiles and laughter to all who passed. An aspiring guitarist, lacking slightly in rhythm but not in enthusiasm, played Wham, Slade and Mariah Carey hits to a cheerful audience who dropped change at regular intervals. Children bounced around their parents with more energy and excitement than ever as the big day loomed less than 24 hours away.

But not every child. Johnny Jarkire barely noticed any of the happiness around him, his eyes and ears switched off, effectively in battery saving mode. He just wanted to get out of the cold, away from everyone, and indeed from himself.

A child of seven knocked Johnny slightly to the ground as she dodged a snowball. He wasn't hurt as he was nudged gently into the snow by the girl who half fell on top of him.

"I'm so sorry," she said genuinely as she shook the snow off of his coat and kindly helped him back upright. She smiled at him. "You can help me get back at my brother if you like. I could use the help." As if to prove the point, she was hit by another snowball, something that made her smile in affection even as she started making another snowball, which she then threw with fiery accuracy.

Johnny tried his best to smile back with the same genuine warmth as the girl but those who have been unhappy will know the difference. He assured her that he was fine and, to the disappointment of the girl, he walked away. She carried on making snowballs, thinking he would look back, but he didn't.

Johnny was also seven, but with the weight of the world around him. He had his hands in his pockets and looked down as he walked away. He was having a hard time at school, where his grades were dropping as he was struggling to concentrate and stay motivated. Why bother knowing about large numbers or learn to spell long words he would never use? He just wanted to be home. Not his current home, but the home he had just left. His old home where he had loads of friends and knew and loved everything about that big city.

Dwayne's Café, where he always got a lemonade with an apple pie every Monday after school. The den behind the park, where he did his skateboard tricks and impressed passers-by on weekends and long summers. His treehouse, where he did his reading and tried out his magic tricks without being disturbed. The basketball team he had helped to win the trophy the year before.

Johnny had moved to this "new adventure" a few weeks ago with his parents after his dad had got promoted at work. In a long chat his dad told him it was a big opportunity and he couldn't turn it down. It was an exciting opportunity, his dad said, as he beamed with pride recounting how he had been specially chosen.

"Sport (that's what his dad always called him), there are 29 people in the office. And they wanted me for the promotion. Little old me. I had no idea. You could have knocked me down with a pile of feathers. I know it's tough to move, but your mother and I have discussed it and it's too good to turn down. We know it's really difficult to leave here, but you'll make new and better friends. I know you will do me proud, Sport."

Adults just don't get it sometimes, thought Johnny. Promotion would be a new car or bigger office. More time off. How can having to get up and move somewhere new be a reward? The kind-hearted boy didn't say anything after an initial protest lasting a few days. His dad had been miserable for months before then. Well, both of his parents, really. They had been arguing so much. They waited until he had gone to bed but he could still hear their raised voices. His dad promised it would be a fresh start and everything would be fine.

And they weren't arguing anymore. Not since the move actually. His dad was working more hours but liking his new job, and his mum was doing well working her language service from home. But their unhappiness had now swapped over to him. Johnny hadn't made any new friends and didn't know where to start. He felt like he had arrived at a cinema where the film had already started and nobody wanted to be interrupted. And now it was Christmas, the film had got to the best part.

His parents had asked for a list to send to Santa a while back. He'd put a few things down, but he'd kept one item off the list as he wanted to earn the money for it himself. There was a magic box set that had made his heart jump. Johnny had some books about magic but this was the one that he dreamed of. It not only had some tricks to try out, it also had the history of magic, with special sections about the most famous magicians written by a modern-day magician who had been inspired by them. There had been a shop that had been selling it. He could feel his heart rate go faster when he held it. If it had that much power just from the box, imagine how much it had inside. Johnny even started to wonder what his magic name would be. He'd been thinking about it and he liked The Mysterious Maestro.

Johnny could totally picture it. He would wear a mask and a cloak and talk with a loud, booming voice. Very different to his regular life. He was pretty shy. Teachers would ask questions and even if he did know the answer, he didn't want to put his hand up. All the other kids staring at him while he answered. It was easier to let someone else answer it.

He walked through the door quietly, but his mother still heard him. There was no need for a burglar alarm. His mum had the hearing of a superhero. She'd heard him countless times, opening a can of soft drinks or a bag of sweets soon before dinner. There was no getting past her.

She stood up in alarm as she looked at her watch. "Oh Johnny, what happened? Why didn't you call? I'd have picked you up. You can't be walking back alone. Don't ever do that again! Did you not enjoy carolling? Do you want me to have a word with the teacher?"

Bless his mum. She was always very inquisitive, even when she was super busy with work. She was a great mum, really. She had no idea what it was like to move and make a whole new set of friends, though. She felt with time, everything could be solved. Johnny just didn't feel like going to the party afterwards. He didn't have anyone to talk to.

"It's ok," Johnny said as he took off his coat and shoes. It really was wonderfully warm in the house. "It wasn't far. And I won't do it again."

"Johnny, you have to understand..."

He was up the stairs and in his room before she had finished. With school over a few days ago and now carolling done, there was no need to do any homework or study of any kind. That was something. He would watch some TV before dinner. He went through the channels, but a lot of them just had Christmas films. Joy everywhere. Instead, he put his headphones on and listened to some loud music. Escape was nice.

And escape was always nicer with Ruffles, a brown and white Australian Shepherd whose hair ruffled when he ran. He really was the best dog ever. He'd wanted one before, but his parents said their house was too small and it was right by a busy road with no parks anywhere near.

But about three weeks before the big move he was out with his mum when he saw a dog by itself lying on the ground making a whimpering noise. His mother had ended the phone call she was on and they looked around to see if he belonged to anyone. But there was no collar, no chip and the dog seemed all alone. They carried him to the vet, where everyone was super nice and they were able to remove the long nail in his paw. What struck Johnny was how intelligent the dog was, like he knew straight away they were there to help him, and the more still he kept, the easier it would be to remove it.

"We'll look after him until the owner comes back for him," said Johnny. Over the next few days, Johnny helped his parents put up posters and asked around with neighbours and local shops, but no one seemed to know who the dog belonged to.

And in this time, his new companion never left his side. They'd go for long walks, play hide and seek and he would hide the treats in different places. They'd race after a ball or a frisbee Johnny had thrown. Ruffles would play in piles of leaves Johnny had pulled together and then they'd make leaf angels. When they got both tired and came back indoors, Johnny would do his magic tricks with Ruffles acting as both his glamorous assistant and impressed audience. Johnny bought him some toys. Even if he was only going to look after him for a short time, he was going to make it a great time for him.

Johnny's mother had told him his owner was bound to claim him back but Johnny was getting more and more attached, even though he kept telling himself that he wasn't. He'd try and keep busy with his homework or chores or practicing his three pointers on his basketball hoop. But he finally admitted to himself one day that Ruffles made him happy and he was glad nobody had claimed him. They went to the nearby park to celebrate and by the way Ruffles ran more excitedly than ever before, it was like he knew.

And today was Christmas Eve. It was nice to look out the window and see snow. It really was pretty and Johnny took some photographs. But he didn't want to go outside again. What was the point? There was nobody he wanted to run into.

Try as he would, he just couldn't get too excited. He might not go outside but he couldn't escape Christmas. His parents were like big kids, so the house and its front entrance were full off Christmas spirit. Outside there were huge, over the top decorations. Along with big flashing lights, there were Santa's feet and a sleigh coming out of the chimney, along with some decorative reindeer, polar bears, penguins, snow leopards and snowy owls.

When his mum protested that not all of those animals were in the North Pole, his dad smiled. "They like the cold," he reasoned. "Besides, it's Christmas. It's a festive hibernation."

The indoor was just as spectacular. The huge Christmas tree had seven different colours and the largest angel Johnny had ever seen. His dad had bought a new one, to go along with the tree. His mum always said his dad got carried away with Christmas, but she had put cards on a string covering wall to wall and always ensured there was Christmas music on and tinsel everywhere in the house. She'd even encouraged his dad to do some baking with her. Though Johnny wasn't too hungry, he could see the gingerbread men were well made.

There didn't seem to be any obvious reason to stay up late, so Johnny was in bed by 9.30. His parents had finally finished working, so they were keen to play a board game or talk about the excitement of tomorrow, but Johnny just wanted to go to sleep and forget Christmas.

"Well ok, son," said his mum, a little surprised. "As long as you have your energy for tomorrow. I bet plenty of wishes will come true tomorrow."

Johnny's only wish was to go back home, but he didn't say anything.

He lay in bed but he knew he wasn't going to sleep, so he took out his book on Houdini. Houdini really was incredible. He could escape from anything. He was such a gifted showman. All the police and people at the time would keep tying him up and he would always find ways to escape. He was just brilliant. Johnny wanted to be like him one day. Not doing card tricks but big events in front of big crowds.

He must have fallen asleep because he woke up a few hours later when he heard unusual noises coming from the window.

He could see Ruffles on his hind legs looking outside. He looked at his watch, but the screen was blank. That was odd. He looked at his alarm clock, but the screen was blank too. That had never happened before. It was working fine last night. He looked up at the window where the sounds were coming from. He couldn't believe it. There was Santa Claus. And a sleigh. And all the reindeer. In *his* back garden. He rubbed his eyes and tapped his cheek but when he looked back out again, they were still there.

But not quite as he would have imagined it. Santa Claus was on the ground, rubbing his back and struggling to stand up.

Johnny quickly opened his window and used the long and thick branches from the tree outside to climb down. Ruffles was able to do the same. Johnny was in his pyjamas and it was cold, but he didn't wait. Santa tried moving, but that only seemed to make the pain worse. It was at that moment that he looked up to see Johnny. "Woah, young man. What are you doing up? It's Christmas Eve. You should be asleep."

Johnny was amazed how deep Santa's voice was. He'd never heard anything like it. It was as though ice could speak. His red cheeks were getting redder as he waited for an answer, but it was clear he couldn't move.

"You should be in be..." His pain was so much that he couldn't even finish his sentence.

Johnny went to see if he could help, but Santa instead pointed to his majestic red sleigh that glimmered as though it had been cleaned by angels. Johnny couldn't see exactly what Santa wanted, but he climbed onto it and saw a small bottle of pills. He brought it along with a small bottle of water that was next to it.

Santa sat up and took a tablet, but it would take a while to work. The reindeer were getting impatient.

Johnny looked at him and then at the shed at the bottom of the garden. "I can't leave you here. Let me help you up to the shed. It's cold, but there's a heater and a chair for when dad gets tired after gardening."

Santa tried to resist, but he was too weak.

Going very slowly, Johnny was able to get him to go the shed. While Ruffles had been interested in the reindeer, he still followed them to the shed. With a heavy sigh and slow movements, Santa sat down and it was clear he wasn't going to be moving much. Johnny switched the heater on and handed him the book he thought Santa would like most. It was on cooking. Santa put it down while he talked to him.

"My back is worse than ever. You're going to have to go to the North Pole for me," Santa said with a sigh. "There's no time to waste. You must go now, Johnny."

Johnny hadn't introduced himself, but Santa laughed. "Of course I know who you are. My back may be creaking but I would never forget a child's name. Even when they move across the country."

Johnny was about to reply, but Santa cut him off with that booming voice of his.

"There's only one trip left and I can't do it. I can't let the children down. I won't let them down. All you have to do is go my home and pick up the last batch of toys and come back. By that time, the pill will have worked."

"I don't even..." started Johnny, but Santa's booming voice spoke with authority. "You have to do it, Johnny. I know you can do it."

Johnny could barely believe his ears. He was being asked to go to the North Pole. The place with the most magic on Earth. Where so many dreams were made.

"Johnny, you have to go now," Santa said, interrupting his thoughts in a soft but firm voice. "The reindeer will guide you."

Johnny opened the door and turned back to ask another question. What about Ruffles? He wanted to take him, but he was having such a great time with Santa. It was as though they had met before. At least Santa would have company.

As if they were listening in, the reindeer made an impatient huffing sound and though he had his back to them, he felt a snowball hit him. Turning around, there were only eight reindeer and then Rudolph out in front. It couldn't have been one of them. Could it?

"Johnny!"

The boy turned round.

"Don't forget the sack!"

Despite its size, it felt very light, so he was able to carry it easily. Johnny looked in, but he wasn't able to see the bottom. Johnny was nervous, but he was ready. He got in the sleigh. It was so big he couldn't even see out over it . It was as if the reindeer understood and they were prepared to take extra control. With a jolt that felt like they were being sent off by a rocket, they were moving and within seconds were up in the air.

Johnny held the reins, but it felt unnecessary. The reindeer knew where they were going, leaving him to enjoy looking down on the world that was getting smaller and smaller with every second. It was faster than anything he could compare it to. It was so much fun.

The view was incredible. He could see all the stars; he could reach out and touch them if he wanted to. He never really noticed before how many there were. Johnny could see the tops of the houses, covered in big and bright decorations. It was like other people had seen his parents' house and felt they could do better. And it was wonderful.

He had no idea how high he was. He didn't even feel the cold, which was odd as there was snow everywhere.

He didn't know how long the journey lasted. His watch was still blank and, above the sky, it was like time didn't exist. There were places without snow and all different kinds of houses. And different stretches of water. How could you be thinking about time when you had the world to look at?

And then suddenly, there was a slight jolt and they were on land. Or at least snow. And he had to rub his eyes again. Sticking out of the snow was a sign saying, "Santa Clause's home", next to a pretty-looking house.

As he was stuck staring at the huge house, he felt a nudge on his shoulder. It was Rudolph. Rudolph's nose was redder than ever and though he seemed happy, he kept on nudging the starstruck boy.

"Okay, okay, Rudolph, I'm getting to it," said Johnny and he jumped out of the sleigh. He knew it was important, so he ran into the house, but he stopped when he was properly inside.

Inside, Mrs Claus was hard at work in the kitchen. Goodness, the kitchen was big.

She was baking food for all the elves. There were cakes and biscuits and chocolate eclairs and apple pies and meringues and doughnuts. Candy Canes were everywhere.

"They sure do love their sugar," said Mrs Clause to herself out loud before she turned around and jumped when she saw Johnny.

"My goodness, what on earth are you doing here?" she gasped in huge shock, almost dropping the tray she was holding. "This place isn't meant to be seen. That's why we're so far away from everyone."

She then spoke faster and with more urgency. "And where is Mr Claus? Is he ok? Is he hurt?"

"It's his back," replied Johnny, trying not to get distracted by all the food. It smelt delicious. "He couldn't move much but he said those tablets would help. He's in my dad's shed at the moment."

"Oh yes, I was worried about that," she said concerned. "He does need to do more of those exercises, but has been so busy." She looked at him closer. "So that's why he sent you. Well, we are short of time. We must get running."

And with that, she opened up a small door and called out to the elves. "It's time, elves. The treats are all ready, but first we need to load up the last batch of presents."

Johnny couldn't resist going through the small door. And what he saw amazed him.

There were elves of all different shapes and shades of colour. And they were busy. And organised. They were so fast and joyous. Johnny could even hear them singing:

"We are happy, they'll be happy

So much goodness is coming their way

It makes us happy they'll be happy

With all the toys they'll have to play."

Johnny had never seen so many toys in his life. There were all kinds. Toy cars, paper aeroplanes, dolls of all colours and hairstyles, building blocks, toy cowboys, bikes, cuddly versions of every animal you could think of, board games, jigsaws. Balls from every sport. There were even a set of elves in an electronic section.

Different elves were doing different things. A few were checking the lists with the presents, some were making them, others were putting the items in boxes, or wrapping them.

"Jermain's going to love this," said an elf in a blue blazer as he finished wrapping a game called Thrills, Spills and Drills. "He must have been a really good boy."

"Aaliyah is the lucky one," said another as she wrapped up a blue furry dinosaur. "He's so cute. I wonder what she'll call him."

Johnny could have stayed there all night. The elves were so focused they wouldn't have noticed him. But he was aware that time was going and he had to make sure all the children got their presents. He helped the elves put the presents in the sack. He had no idea it would fit so many, but it seemed to have far more space than your regular sack.

He carried the sack through the kitchen and just had to look around again. It was so big and organised and all the foods smelt delicious. Mrs Claus looked at him and as she ushered him through to the reindeers, she handed him a ham sandwich and a mixture of sugary desserts.

"Thanks for all the treats, Mrs Claus," said a grateful Johnny. He hadn't been hungry until he was in the kitchen but now he could easily eat them all without blinking. He wanted to ask her so many questions. But there wasn't time. So he only asked her the first one he could think of. "Don't you want to ride the sleigh too?"

"Oh goodness, no," she replied with a laugh. "I am already busy enough. You have no idea how exhausted I am by the end of Christmas Eve. As well as baking all the extra sweet things for the elves and preparing the right food for Mr Claus and the reindeers, I help update the list for all the children who have moved in the past year, check the elves are sticking to the schedule and keeping an eye on the time as Mr Claus is always running late."

She looked at her watch. Johnny was desperate to know what time it was, but he wasn't close enough to tell. She didn't need to say anything. Johnny didn't want any child to wake up on Christmas Day without their presents.

And with that, he was off. The reindeer had just finished eating the carrots in front of them and they were ready to go.

If anything, it was like the sleigh was moving faster. Just what was in those carrots? Johnny wondered. He held on tight to the reins, but it didn't stop him appreciating the pretty world underneath him. It was a different set of houses and streets and neighbourhoods. And decorations. So many flashing colours. People just loved Christmas.

Johnny had loved Christmas too. He'd had so many wonderful memories over the years. Playing volley tennis over the snow, singing carols, being a talkative tree in a Christmas play, inventing a new juice drink made from everything liquid in his fridge. It tasted awful, but all of his friends had drunk it and it had brought them closer together. He would never forget those moments. He wondered what they would be asking for Christmas and how much they were missing him.

He started thinking, too, about all the presents going to children around the world. He started picturing their reactions. All that joy, all that happiness. All the different presents. Johnny wondered how many other kids were interested in magic. He hadn't noticed anything at the workshop. Maybe he could inspire those around him. Maybe he could do a magic show. But that would mean talking to new people.

He had no idea where he was or how long it had taken, but he could suddenly feel the sleigh lowering. And it wasn't long before he recognised his neighbourhood and his house coming closer into view.

The landing was perfect. What made it even sweeter was that Santa and Ruffles were waiting to see him.

"I could hear those bells a mile away," said Santa with a hearty grin. Johnny hadn't noticed them at all. "I jumped up as soon as your adorable dog heard them," Santa continued. "And I'm feeling better than ever. Half of it is down to the tablet, the other half to this wonderful creature of yours."

Santa had made a new friend for sure.

"But I must get going," he said with a hurried tone. "There are still some presents left to deliver. The children all deserve it and I will never let them down. I don't know how I could thank you enough, Johnny."

Johnny had been so distracted by the views he still hadn't eaten the sandwich which Mrs Claus had kindly made for him. Or any of the slices of cake, small doughnuts or apple pie. "Here, you must be starving. Mrs Claus made it for me but you can have it."

There seemed to be an extra sparkle in the eyes of Santa Claus as he replied. "I've eaten plenty, my dear boy. Mrs Claus always has things so well organised. I'd be lost without her help. It doesn't surprise me she made that sandwich even with all the things she has going on. Her kindness was one of the things that I first noticed about her. She was tending to a sick reindeer even though she had her bag of shopping and it was pouring with rain. She's very special."

This whole evening had been pretty incredible. How many children got to see where Santa lived and the elves' workshop?

"Now Johnny, I know you like your magic. So, I know I can count on you not to tell anyone about this. Even when everyone wants to know the secret, a magician can't reveal anything."

"I promise, Santa," said Johnny genuinely.

"I know things have been tough for you with the move. There are times when we're unhappy. Life isn't easy sometimes. But it's getting through those tough times that makes us who we are. There are things to be sad about. But there are even more things to be happy about. And I know you will find all the happiness that there is around you and make it part of you."

And with that Santa was ready to leave. He held out his hand and Johnny shook it. "You stepped up and you've helped ensure a lot of children will get the presents they deserve."

"It's no problem, Santa," replied the boy, smiling. He hadn't smiled like that in months.

And with that, Santa and his sleigh were off. But one of the presents had fallen out. He shouted but there was no way Santa would be able to hear him. Johnny started moving his arms in big motions and jumping up and down, waving the present around.

He was very lucky as, just as they were about to quickly launch higher with a faster speed, they had seen him and spun around. Within seconds they were back on the ground.

"My goodness, that would have been horrible for little Antoine," said Santa without even looking at the gift tag. "He's been such a great kid this year. I can't believe that present fell out. I have such large pockets on this outfit. Usually when something falls out, it's in there."

"Are you sure you're going to be ok, Santa?" said Johnny, a little worried.

"My boy, I'll be fine. But I do need to get going. Don't forget what I said. By making others happy, you can find a happiness within you. People around you will care about you when they get to know you."

The young boy waved and within a second, he was staring at the sky as the sleigh had disappeared from view. And for the first time, he started to feel cold. Ruffles was a dog for all weathers, but he had started to move less and he was barking a little more.

"Let's go inside, boy. And you can have my sandwich." He dropped it to the ground as he climbed up into his room. But how to get Ruffles up? He had a look around, but there was nothing obvious. All he could see was his laundry basket. That could work, though. He'd seen it in movies. He took off his two bedsheets and connected them to either end of his now empty basket. He lowered it down and Ruffles got in. With some strong pulls, Ruffles was soon in the room. Johnny ate what was on the foil and lay down.

He didn't know how long he was asleep. Usually, he was the first one up, but when his mum and dad woke him, they had clearly been up a while. His watch and alarm clock were working.

"Wakey wakey, Sport," said his excited father, dressed in a jumper with a big red reindeer on the front. "You know what day it is today! Get on up, sleepyhead."

"You must have been tired!" said his mother. "Your sheets are all over the place!"

"You need to get a move on," said his father who was almost bouncing off the walls. "Presents time. I wanted to wake you up earlier, but your mum said we should let you sleep."

"Okay okay, he'll be ready soon" said his mum as she quietly moved his dad out of the room. "Such a big kid," she whispered to Johnny with a big smile.

It certainly had been a quick start to the day and it had barely started. Could he have dreamt the whole thing? Helping Santa Claus, being on the sleigh, meeting the elves and Mrs Claus. That couldn't be. He looked out of the window almost in case the sleigh was there. Or at least some proof it was. But there was nothing.

Maybe it was just a dream, he reasoned. It was a happy one, anyhow. Things felt different. He felt different.

And if everyone was in a film and he was late, well, Johnny would make that work. Plenty of films had interesting characters appear midway through. Maybe there was a basketball club? And if there wasn't one, well it was about time he started one. He knew his parents would help him. Maybe that snowball girl would play.

He got dressed and went downstairs. His mum was getting the food for Ruffles. All the presents were there just waiting to be opened. His name was on so many. He could even see one for Ruffles. It looked like a new frisbee. At that moment, his dad came in wearing a novelty Christmas hat and a puzzled expression.

"It's the strangest thing. I went to the shed just now to get my reindeer hat and there was this present. It's for Johnny."

His dad handed it over. Johnny checked the label. "To Johnny. You deserve this for everything you've done. From Santa."

It was a differently shaped present to the ones under the tree. He could barely lift it. Like it was a big set of things. And it felt like magic.

Background Notes

The Prankster

It was always going to be the first story of this collection. I was tempted to call it "Jimmy Nirvana" but "The Prankster" was a better reflection of the story. The idea came to me after I read about a mean-spirited prank and the fallout from it. I was intrigued by the motivations of the person behind it and just ran with it.

Lies and Secrets

I wrote this story while at sixth form college, after thinking how awkward it would be to run into an ex-girlfriend. The temptation was to modernise it adding social media references, but it just seemed to alter the rhythm and context of the story.

Lucky/Unlucky

This story developed from several ideas. What would happen if the circumstances of your name changed overnight and it became a punchline? What's a funny way for a couple to meet? Is there such thing as fate?

That Beautiful Girl

I grew up watching MTV and was always curious if I could come up with an original idea for a music video. I didn't make that video but I did write up the story. Reading it back years later I kept most of it, but made several slight changes; mostly in the dialogue.

Motive, Murder, Method

Shows like *Alfred Hitchcock Presents* and *Tales of the Unexpected* always appealed to me and one of the more common themes is of the main character's desperation to kill off their spouse. It tied in with an idea I had about a nice guy with an unexciting life who isn't quite the person everyone else thinks he is.

There, Unthere

This was the first story I wrote after *The Summer of Madness* and I set out to make it as different as possible. The title comes from my favourite Radiohead song "There, There". If you look carefully, you'll even spot a song lyric I included.

The Magic of Christmas

I had never previously written anything set during Christmas. It's such a wonderful time of the year but that doesn't mean we're at our happiest. This story conveys the message that when there is magic in the air, good things really can happen.

Printed in Dunstable, United Kingdom

71022587R00077